BURNT EMBERS

a novel by

D. F. Bailey

Burnt Embers
Copyright © D. F. Bailey 2023
ISBN: 978-1-990646-10-2

Burnt Embers is a work of fiction. The resemblance of any character to real persons, living or dead, is coincidental. All names, characters, places, brands, media, situations, and incidents are the product of the author's imagination or used fictitiously.

Subscribe to D. F. Bailey's newsletter: www.dfbailey.com

A Gathering of Angels

The Madness of Men

A World on Fire

"Without order, nothing can exist.
Without chaos, nothing can evolve."
— *Oscar Wilde*

CHAPTER ONE

ON THURSDAY, THE day before the Gathering of Angels conference, Eve Noon chuckled when she and Will Finch first entered the Rotunda of the Big River Resort and Conference Center.

"Maybe the word *Rotunda* is a tad grandiose, don't you think?" she whispered. She covered her mouth with a hand to ensure that the center staff wouldn't hear the jibe. "After all, this isn't exactly the US Capitol dome."

"No. Not quite." Will Finch's face widened into a broad grin as he rolled their suitcases along the corridor and stood on the lip of the dome entrance. Despite the five balloons floating under the ceiling, the round, open space radiated with warmth, light, and natural elegance. "Too bad someone added the helium balloons."

"SVB." She pointed to the logos on the balloons. "Silicon Valley Bank. Our biggest sponsor."

"I guess someone has to pay for the bells and whistles. Might as well be a bank."

They took a moment to admire the dome which rose twenty

feet above them. Constructed from narrow cedar beams configured in identical, equilateral triangles, the meeting space felt like a mathematical marvel. The triangles were bolted together to form hexagons that were covered with a synthetic fiber that looked like weathered birch bark. The ground-level hexagons served as window frames that offered a sweeping view of the surrounding forest.

As requested by Eve, the room was set up with five rows of chairs facing a raised dais that held a lectern and a multimedia tech rack equipped with a laptop and audio-video equipment.

"Wow. It's brilliant," Eve said to Finch. "I'm really glad that Roland talked me into hosting the conference here."

Roland Clapp, the resident manager of the Big River Resort, couldn't be more proud of the hidden gem. Clapp had stood at the doorway to greet Eve and Finch when they drove up the gravel driveway to the resort entrance. He wore a checked lumberman's jacket, khaki jeans, and a tattered pair of hiking boots. A tall, lean man, he sported a trim salt-and-pepper beard. His smile suggested he'd just heard a clever joke. Woodsy, Finch thought. And eager to please.

After they checked in, Clapp guided them through the resort dining room, the Swedish sauna and spa, the bar, and the lounge. His tour concluded at the Rotunda room.

"While he didn't invent it, Buckminster Fuller patented the geodesic dome in 1954," he said, his voice rising with a reverent authority. "Ask any architect and they'll say Fuller was a modern-day Renaissance man. His work inspired a flood of post-modern building designs around the world. Including this diamond in the woods." Clapp raised his hand to the ceiling as if he were introducing them to a cherished friend.

"You're right." Finch had often admired Fuller's work. "This is a lovely surprise."

"Well, I'll let you explore the rest of the facilities on your own," Clapp said. He turned to Eve. "So tomorrow evening the conference kicks off. Still have thirty-two delegates, or did some drop out?"

"No, thirty-two it is. But you never know."

"No problem. And we have room for more if you need the space. Later-comers are better than no-shows. Let's review the arrangements tomorrow after breakfast if you like."

"Perfect."

Clapp pointed to the exterior pathway. "Your cottage, the Sugar Pine, is at the far end of the trail. Our little hideaway. No one will know you're there," he added with a wink.

Finch appreciated the gesture. He needed a vacation. Last month Eve talked him into joining her at the corporate conference. The so-called "Gathering of Angels" was her idea for a meet-and-greet getaway weekend where so-called angel investors — high-risk money managers — could identify investable media startups. Over the past decade, San Francisco had become saturated with big ideas looking for big money. By isolating both parties in the remote forest away from the city Eve could provide the time and distance for everyone to make well-considered assessments.

At first, Finch hesitated. He didn't much care for corporate movers and shakers. Their empires, driven by bleeding-edge technology and fueled by mergers and acquisitions, often resulted in staff layoffs and downsizing. Ten years ago, he'd salvaged his budding journalism career when Wally Gimbel, the managing editor of *The San Francisco Post*, offered him a position as a crime reporter when the digital wing of the paper was carved off from the once-thriving daily edition. Then Eve purchased the last surviving piece of the business and turned it into a break-even media hub. By today's standards, *The Post* was an astonishing success story.

Her role as conference facility coordinator was to find an outstanding venue that was remote — yet accessible — to California's media moguls. The Big River Resort and Conference Center was definitely outstanding and certainly remote. But accessible? Eve knew most conference delegates would balk at the three-hour drive from San Francisco along the serpentine coast highway to Mendocino. Then Roland Clapp suggested that the delegates fly to the Mendocino Bay float-plane dock. Eve became intrigued. Everyone could wing in on their floatplanes and show off their latest toys. She'd pitch the journey as a new adventure for some of the most venturesome entrepreneurs in America. Another notch on their belts.

The day before the conference kickoff, Eve and Finch chartered a floatplane to Mendocino Bay, then rented a car. They drove to the nearest village — Mendocino, a celebrated artist colony that served as Cabot Cove, Maine, the setting for the popular TV series, *Murder She Wrote.* They ate lunch at one of the hipster restaurants overlooking the Pacific Ocean, then drove out of town along East Oak Street. A mile later the paved road became a gravel track through the tinder-dry forest that was parched from the enduring drought. After driving another thirty miles they reached the lodge, a rural hideaway tucked between Pudding Creek and Big River.

Following their tour of the conference facilities with Clapp, Finch dragged the twin suitcases along the path to the Sugar Pine cottage. When he unlocked the door, Eve stepped past him, held her arms aloft, and swung around in a girlish pirouette.

"Ohhh, Will. This *is* special." She walked into the bathroom and examined the vanity, the soaker tub, the terry cloth bathrobes and towels.

She swung back into the bedroom and opened the drapes that covered the French doors. Finch slung the suitcases onto the king bed and shuffled next to her. He wrapped both arms around her waist and snuggled her against his chest. She settled into the warmth of his body and let out a gentle purr. Their fingers wove together as they swayed slowly in place while they gazed through the glass doors. The view looked into a wilderness of massive redwood trees.

"You think Big River's down there someplace?"

"Maybe."

She turned out of his arms to survey the rest of the cottage. "Okay, so two special things about this place." She kissed his cheek.

"Yeah? Like what?"

"One, no TV. Which means no distractions. Two, that little acorn stove with a stack of presto logs ready to burn."

He knew what she was thinking.

"Now if you were to make a fire while I take a bath and then change into something, uh, special … I wonder what might happen. Don't you?"

"Gee, I dunno." He put on an innocent look. "Maybe I should see if I can scrounge up a box of matches and find out."

"Okay." A smile. "You do that while I freshen up." She slipped into the bathroom and closed the door.

Freshen up. He chuckled at that. Eve loved to set the mood with her bedroom eyes and a come-and-get-me grin.

He could hear water streaming into the tub while he searched the coffee table drawers between two wingback chairs. Ah, there. A small box of wooden match sticks lay next to a deck of playing cards. The label read *Compliments of Big River Resort.* He pushed the sliding box open with his index finger. Full. Not one stick missing. He lit the fireplace with one match and slipped the box into the watch pocket in his jeans. A keepsake, he thought. To remember another special night with Eve in his arms.

CHAPTER TWO

EVE NOON'S EYES blinked open when she heard the first thunderclap rumble through the room. Or was it the second? She took a moment to find her bearings. Right, they were sleeping in the Sugar Pine cottage. In the last log cabin down the chip trail from the resort. She checked the bedside clock. 2:17 AM, Saturday.

It was their second night, and they'd been late getting to bed. All the conference delegates had gathered for the opening meet-n-greet reception. The four-course meal had been followed by an open bar and one too many champagne fizzes which continued to buzz through her head.

When another crash sounded, she sat upright and pulled the blankets to her chest. *A thunderstorm?* She shook her head. No, something else. Something is very wrong.

"Will? You hear that?"

"Whaaa?" His feet stirred under the bedcovers.

She brushed a hand over his shoulder. "The front door."

When two more blows struck the door, Finch sat bolt upright, his heart thudding in his chest.

"Fire!" A man's baritone voice bellowed into the cabin.

"What the hell?" His feet dropped to the floor and he found his way to the wall next to the bathroom where they'd hung their clothes on the row of wooden pegs. No closets here. According to Eve, the decor was intentionally minimalist. "Wilderness chic," she called it

"Turn on the light," he mumbled. "I can't find my pants."

"Emergency!" a panicked voice barked. "We got a wildfire break-out up the valley."

Eve clicked on the bedside table lamp and watched her husband tug on his pants and shirt. "It's almost two-thirty," she moaned. "Who is it?"

"God knows," he grumbled and crossed the plank floor. He sniffed the air, testing for any scent of fire. The embers in the acorn stove still glowed from the fire he'd lit earlier in the evening. The second fire, two nights in a row. But smoke? No, not a whiff of it.

"Who's there?"

"Forest fire! Everyone's gotta evacuate right now!"

"Forest fire?" Eve pulled her robe from the armchair next to the sliding glass doors and tugged it over her shoulders. She tied the cloth belt across her waist and hoisted her suitcase onto the ottoman. "We need to grab everything."

Finch felt a ripple of hesitation as he reached the cabin door. No spy hole, he thought and latched the security chain across the doorframe. He cracked the door open, then the chain snapped away and the door crashed into him. As he tried to turn away, the door edge slashed his forehead above his right eyebrow.

"What the fu — " he whined and stumbled into the living room.

"Will! Watch out!"

Before she could reach him, he crashed to the floor and smacked his elbow against the arm of the sofa.

"God damn it!" he cried and grasped the elbow in the palm of his hand.

Two men stormed into the cabin. They wore matching desert camo fatigues and black balaclava masks. Each mask had three holes, two for the eyes, one for the mouth.

"Try to get up and I'll put you down hard," the first man barked. He swung a truncheon in his right hand and raised it above his left shoulder, poised to strike into Finch's skull.

Finch held a hand to his forehead. A trickle of blood seeped onto his cheek.

"He's bleeding," Eve whimpered and knelt next to her husband.

The second man studied Finch's face. "It's nothin'," he muttered. "Now get dressed. We gotta move. Fast."

"What?" Finch blinked three or four times to clear the haze from his eyes.

When he was able to focus he noticed the hand clenching the truncheon. The tips of all four fingers were missing. All cut off at an angle. Stubs. His partner stared at Finch as if he were assessing the damage to Finch's head. Even in the midnight shadows, his steel blue eyes radiated a penetrating gaze.

"Get yourself dressed, bitch. In there," Blue Eyes said to Eve as his head swiveled toward the bathroom. "Make it quick."

Get dressed? Eve shook her head in confusion. "All right." She took a moment to gather her clothes, shoes, and a fleece jacket. The realization that they didn't intend to rape her provided some relief. Relief undercut by the thought they were planning something worse.

"Now!" he yelled when he saw her hesitate. He grabbed her forearm and shoved her toward the bathroom.

"All right!" Eve wheeled her arm free from his grasp and closed the bathroom door behind her. What the hell? These crazies meant business. But what now? she mumbled to herself as she tugged on her clothes. They could really hurt Will. And make a total mess of her.

When she opened the door she saw both men leaning forward as they examined Will's face. The trickle of blood was now a steady stream rolling onto his shirt.

"Got a first aid kit in there?" Blue Eyes notched his head back toward the bathroom.

"I think I've got something."

"All right. Patch him up."

"And make it fast, bitch," the first man added. "This thing's on the clock."

On the clock? Finch wondered what they were up against. This was no random B and E, snatch-and-grab. He pressed the palm of his hand to his forehead. He'd taken a hell of a wallop, but he hadn't blacked out. With luck, there'd been no concussion.

Finch looked at his tormentor — Stubs — and tried to detect a hint of sympathy in his eyes. "I'm just going to sit up, okay?"

Stubs looked like he held nothing but contempt for Finch. The truncheon was still poised to strike him.

Finch held up a hand to ward off any blows. "Just gonna lean against the sofa. Okay?"

"Just 'til she fixes you. But try somethin', and I'll put you down for keeps."

Will waved his free hand, palm out, to suggest he understood. He focused his eyes on the cudgel. A leather strap attached to the club was looped around his wrist. Despite his missing fingertips, Finch knew this bruiser could do a lot of damage. Both men stood at least six feet tall and looked fighting fit.

When Stubs offered no objections, Finch braced himself with his left hand and eased his back up along the side of the sofa. His head began to pulse with pain. To distract himself he watched Blue Eyes scoop their cell phones and the keys to the rental car from the top of the coffee table and drop them into a shopping bag.

"Any other phones?" he asked.

"No," Finch muttered. "Just the two."

Eve returned from the bathroom with her cosmetic bag and a damp washcloth. In addition to her cosmetics, she always carried some basic first aid supplies when they were traveling. Alcohol swabs, steri-strips, painkillers, compresses.

"I gotta get down beside him, okay?"

Stubs nodded and turned his attention to Blue Eyes. "Call up Skipper. Tell him we'll be there in ten."

As Blue Eyes spoke on his Icom two-way radio, Eve

zipped open the cosmetic bag and kneeled on the floor in front of her husband. Finch spread his legs so she could squat between them. She inched forward to examine his wound and dabbed the blood from his face with the washcloth. "Looks okay. About two inches long," she murmured. "You might need a stitch or two, but this'll do for now."

She tore open an alcohol swab foil. Finch let out a light gasp as she dragged the disinfectant over the laceration. Then she opened a box of steri-strips and pulled out a few bandaids.

"Hold this," she whispered and pressed the packet into his hand. Then she peeled off the backing of four, inch-long strips and strapped them across the gash on his forehead in a ladder that climbed from his eyebrow to his hairline. After she closed the wound, she studied his face for a moment.

"Looks like that staunched the bleeding. At least for now." She leaned closer. "You feel okay?"

"Yeah."

When he realized that Eve had blocked Stubs's view of his face, Finch pressed his chin forward and began to mouth some instructions to her. "*You have to escape.*" He paused to ensure that she grasped what he was saying. "*Understand? Escape,*" he repeated.

She nodded once and whispered, "Don't worry. I'll do it."

"Cut the chitty-chat," Stubs commanded. "Get his shoes on, then we head out."

He leaned over to the doormat and tossed Finch's Nikes to her.

After she tied the trainers to his feet, she said, "Okay, we're good to go."

At least they had a plan, she thought. This would be her part of it. To escape and find help. But where? They were thirty miles from the coast and Mendocino. Did they even have a cop station in the village? She let out a sigh of exasperation. Maybe she could find someone living in the surrounding forest. Or somewhere along the river.

CHAPTER THREE

BLUE EYES AND Stubs led Eve and Finch into the Rotunda Room, the primary meeting venue at the center. The overhead lights had been dimmed and the Silicon Valley Bank helium balloons swayed against the pennant banners strung across the top of the geodesic dome. The neatly arranged conference chairs and tables had been shoved willy-nilly onto the stage, and the staff and convention delegates squatted on the floor and leaned against the glass windows that formed a circular wall. Roland Clapp, the center manager, huddled beside the arched doorway leading into the resort reception area, lounge, and dining hall. Clapp held a hand to his face and as Finch and Eve were prodded into the room by Stubs, Finch detected a bruise swelling on Clapp's left cheek. He'd suffered a blow to the head, too. Finch offered him a cursory nod, but Clapp appeared too dazed to respond.

"Keep moving," Blue Eyes commanded, dragging Eve forward by her elbow and pushing her onto the floor next to the fire exit.

Finch sat beside her and tried to assess their situation. The conference delegates and their partners huddled on the floor around the circumference of the dome. Eve had introduced him to most of them a few hours earlier at the meet-and-greet soirée. Thirty-two men and women, but no children. All the delegates with families had left their children at home. Eve's and Will's daughter Casey was staying with Eve's sister in Berkeley. Thank God, he whispered to himself.

He counted three men and a woman striding back and forth in front of the cowed hostages. All four wore combat fatigues and balaclavas. Handguns, truncheons, and multitools hung from their belts. They all had modified AR-15s strapped behind their shoulders. Stubs stopped and swayed from foot to foot in front of Finch and the two prisoners hunched on the floor beside him. Did Stubs and Blue Eyes have the rifles when they'd abducted them? Finch couldn't remember. They'd had billy clubs, but the AR-15s? He pressed the ball of his hand to his forehead. Dull shockwaves blazed through his skull. He tried to ease the worst of it by focusing his mind on the epicenter of pain. When he couldn't bear another moment, he shuddered with a heavy gasp.

"You okay?" Eve whispered.

"Yeah. I'll make it."

"No talking!" One of their captors pointed his fist at Eve, then turned and walked in a tight circle in the middle of the room. "That goes for everyone," he barked. Unlike the others who wore desert sand camo, his was forest green. He waved a hand to one of the men next to the double doors where Roland Clapp sat.

"Dogboy, close the door."

So Blue Eyes's nickname was Dogboy. Finch recalled the nicknames he'd heard during his years stationed in Iraq. Dogboy likely referred to a dumb grunt who could be counted on to dig through hell to complete his mission. Dogboy's only distinguishing feature was the military tattoo on his left hand. Otherwise, he stood just under six feet and looked well-built and fit.

"Yes, Skipper."

Skipper. The name usually referred to a small vessel captain, a yachtsman who loved to fish. But not this dude. Not a chance. Another six-footer, he bore the thick neck of a Greco-Roman wrestler trained to grind his opponents into submission.

Dogboy pulled the swing doors together and turned the deadbolt to lock them in place. He then stood in ready position, feet braced a foot apart to block any escape attempts.

Skipper turned to Stubs. "Claws, run a headcount."

Claws. The perfect name for Stubbs. Despite his headache, Finch let out a bleak chuckle. He watched Claws walk in a circle, his good hand notching up and down as he counted off each of the captives. When he approached Finch, he could see Claws's lips counting. Twenty-seven, twenty-eight... When he completed the circuit he swung around.

"Headcount's thirty-six, Skipper."

Obviously, each of them had a nom de guerre. Skipper, the captain. Dogboy. Claws, a foot soldier. Who was the woman?

"Thirty-six," Skipper repeated. He walked over to Roland Clapp and squatted in front of him. "How many staff on the night shift?"

Clapp, still in a daze from the blow to his head, shrugged as if he didn't understand the question. His wife Jean held his hand and pulled it toward her to rouse him.

Skipper put a hand on Clapp's shoulder and squeezed it. Suddenly he snapped out of his reverie.

"What?"

"I said how many staff are on night shift?"

Clapp blinked and gazed at the ceiling. It looked as if he were counting the paper triangles in the pennant banners strung across the roof. Finally, he muttered, "Uh, three."

"Who?"

Another pause. "The night auditor. The chef. And Michaels."

"Who's Michaels?'

"Head of maintenance. Lives in the backyard A-frame."

Skipper pointed a finger to the floor. "He's here, now?"

"Yes." He nodded to a man dressed in overalls opposite the entry door.

"Who's the night auditor and chef?"

Another pause. Clapp tipped his chin to his immediate left. "Randy Salter's, the night auditor. Finnegan's our chef."

Hunched beside Clapp, the two men appeared to sink a few inches lower onto the floor.

"So including you and your wife, there's just the five of you who run this place in here now?"

"Right." Clapp now appeared fully alert. His fingers daubed at the purple bruise on his left cheekbone.

"And everyone else here is attending the conference?"

He paused to consider the question. "Right."

"How many day staff come on shift in the morning?"

Clapp paused to run another mental calculation. "Nine."

"When do they start?"

"In dribs and drabs. The girls who clean the rooms punch in first. They start at seven."

Skipper checked his watch.

"All right. *Salter.*" He turned to the night auditor and studied his face for a moment. He waited until he knew he had Salter's full attention. "Your job is to contact all the day staff and cancel their shifts for the next three days. Tell them we have a Covid-19 outbreak and they're ordered to stay home until further notice. And tell them the resort will cover their wages. In full. You got that?"

Salter's chin wobbled slightly. The best he could offer was a weak nod.

"I need to hear you say it. *You got it?*"

Another nod. Then, "Yeah. Cancel the day shift. Tell them Covid-19."

"At full wages."

"At full wages," Salter repeated.

"All right. If any of them show up — for any reason — you'll pay for it. *Personally,*" Skipper added so that Salter harbored no doubt he'd pay a heavy price.

"Jasper. Go with him. When he's done, report back.

Jasper, the lone female, marched forward and swung the muzzle of her rifle at Salter's face. Fit and well-built, she stood about five-foot-five but looked as if she'd spent years training in a gym. She kept her hair tucked under the balaclava. Blonde, redhead — who could tell? If push came to shove, Finch knew he didn't want to test himself in a confrontation with her.

"You got it, Skipper." She guided the night auditor through the lobby door and they marched down the hallway to the reception desk.

"All right, everyone else, listen up." Skipper walked in a wide circle in the middle of the room. He clasped a baton in his right hand and tapped it into his left palm. *Whump, whump, whump.* The sound of wood striking flesh matched the rhythm of his slow, steady pace. "Okay, shoes and socks off."

A meek silence settled over the hostages.

"Now!" He screamed and swung the cudgel over the maintenance manager's head. In one, decisive move he could split Michaels's skull in two. "Now!"

Michaels quickly heeled his shoes from his feet and slipped his socks onto the floor.

"Good. Now, everybody. Same goes for every one of you." Skipper wheeled around in a continuously rotating circle. "Shoes and socks off."

As he spoke Finch noticed the lower edge of Skipper's balaclava slip above his bulging larynx. The thick Adam's apple bobbled as if it might choke him.

When everyone had stripped off their socks and shoes, he pointed his baton at Michaels again. "Collect them up." He aimed his club at the crash door where Eve and Finch sat together. "Throw them over there. Out of the way."

It took Michaels almost ten minutes to hobble around the room, gather the shoes and socks, and toss them in front of the steel exit door beside Eve. Fifteen minutes later, the night auditor returned to the Rotunda with Jasper at his side. Salter crouched down at his spot on the floor and Jasper gave a curt nod to Skipper.

"Job done," she reported. "All the day staff are in the loop." Her voice fluttered as if she had to bottle up a shot of anxiety.

"Copy that." Skipper nodded at her and pulled the bottom of his face mask below his throat. Then one by one he pointed to the rest of the resort staff. "Michaels, Finnegan, Salter. The three of you stand up. You too, Mrs. Clapp." When Roland Clapp started to object, Skipper pressed the palm of his hand down over Clapp's head. "You sit. The four of you, follow Jasper."

A brief hesitation ensued as the three staff members studied Jasper and then rose to their feet. When he saw Clapp's wife resisting, Skipper sneered and tugged her away from her husband. He shoved her towards Jasper, who wound her fingers around Jean Clapp's delicate wrist.

"We need sandwiches and coffee. The four of you are on kitchen detail. You need to prepare food for forty. That means sandwiches, tea, coffee, water." The baton beat an easy rhythm in his open palm. *Thuck, thuck.* "Jasper's in charge. You do what she says. And you do it fast with no questions."

He turned his hand in a wide circle to encompass everyone in the room. "Now listen up. I need everyone to understand something."

Skipper leveled his truncheon in the air, then swung around to address all the hostages. "Anything goes wrong in *here,* then one of the staff members dies *in the kitchen.*" He crooked a thumb toward the door. "And any of you staff who fail to follow orders from Jasper" — he notched his fist and pointed at Jasper — *"will result in a death inside this room."*

A collective murmur swelled through the Rotunda as a feeling of bleak hopelessness weighed on everyone.

"I fucking mean it!" Skipper barked and drove the butt of his club into Salter's belly. The night auditor let out a cry and dropped to the floor.

Two or three people shrieked at once, then hushed into a shocked silence when they realized any more complaints would result in random punishments. Maiming, killing. Who knew what might follow?

"All right. Jasper, take 'em down to the kitchen."

Finnegan braced Salter under his shoulder to help him stand. Then Jasper led the victims toward the hallway. Dogboy shoved the door open and the three employees along with Jean Clapp slipped into the dim corridor that led to the reception desk, dining room, and kitchen.

When the door slammed shut, Finch closed his eyes. He tried to focus. If he could create a distraction, just ten or fifteen seconds that might draw the assailants away, perhaps Eve could break through the emergency exit beside them. The door had a crash bar and if it was unlocked, she could nudge her hip into the bar and slip outside. He tried to recall the exterior surroundings illustrated in the map mounted on the wall above the reception desk. The lodge was encircled by a vast forest. Nothing but dry, parched woods, and somewhere in the distance, Pudding Creek and Big River. Beyond that — on the Pacific coast — the village of Mendocino. Would it work? He shook his head. Likely Skipper and his team had chained the door from the outside. That's what Finch would've done before the hostages were penned in the Rotunda.

After the staff departed, Skipper walked to the stage and signaled Dogboy to stream a video from the projector. As he toyed with the equipment a low murmur resonated amongst the hostages.

The buzz seemed to amuse Skipper. "In a moment you'll have something to talk about." He glanced at Dogboy. "You got it?"

"Yeah. Show time," Dogboy said with a grin. The screen above the podium flashed with amber light for a few seconds then an amateurish title screen appeared in bold, italic red letters.

THE REVOLUTION HAS BEGUN
CLEAR THE MEDIA SCUM FROM THE SWAMP

"Hit the pause button." Skipper pointed his club at Dogboy. When the video stopped, he continued. "In case you don't know, *you're* the media scum" — an arm swept forward to suggest everyone on the floor was contemptible — "the purveyors of the great American disaster."

He turned back to Dogboy and nodded.

"Watch and learn," Skipper commanded as a series of clips appeared on the screen above his head. It began with a scene showing Nancy Greenlaw walking through the doors leading into her office — Media$$ — in San Francisco's Financial District. Then the video cut to her playing with her two daughters in her front yard in Tiburon.

"Hey! What the — " she gasped.

"Button your mouth, bitch," Dogboy growled. "This is just

the beginning for you. For all of you," he added.

Similar scenes followed. Barry Bigalow, CEO of Profound Sounds, as he ordered a round of cocktails at a tennis club with his girlfriend, Ainsley. Jeff Sconce from Tite-Flite Digital, picking up his son in his shiny, white Tesla from the driveway of his ex-wife, Sonia. Frank Winters and his trophy wife, Jeanine, dressed up as Dick and Liz Burton at the MiniMax Digital Media Halloween party. Each sequence named the individuals, their businesses, and home addresses. The eleventh clip introduced Will and Eve.

A still photo grabbed from *The Post* website showed Eve addressing her Board of Directors meeting. Finch was captured in TV interviews on CNN and PBS promoting his latest book, *White Sphere: The Dark Side of the Pandemic.*

The closing shot showed them tossing a baseball to their daughter Casey at the neighborhood park in Berkeley.

Eve clasped Will's hand. His head throbbed with pain and sheer outrage. It took him a moment to clamp down his fury.

"God help us," she whispered.

His jaw tightened. Better not to let these bandits hear a word. "You have to get out of here," he breathed.

"But — "

"No. It's got to be you. You know it."

After another twenty minutes, the opening title reappeared — *THE REVOLUTION HAS BEGUN. CLEAR THE MEDIA SCUM FROM THE SWAMP* — and the video faded in a choppy, digital haze. The silence in the room felt leaden. Dogboy cut the video and closed the laptop while Skipper took to the stage again. A few people broke into sobs. Most were cowering, covering their eyes hoping to make this nightmare vanish.

"So," Skipper whispered as if it might be a burden to speak to the scum sitting at his feet. "Now you know what this is about. The revolution has started and you" — now his baton swept the air before him in a gentle caress that held them in his thrall — "you are all prisoners of war."

A moment passed, then Claws approached the stage. He held a ledger book in one hand.

"Skipper, we've gotta problem," he said in a muted voice.

"A problem?"

"I just checked the guest register against the head count. So we had thirty-six in here. Right? Now the night staff and Clapp's wife" — he pointed to Clapp who continued to nurse the bruise on his cheek — "are with Jasper. Right? That takes us down to thirty-two."

"So?"

"So it should be thirty-three. Check the register." Claws passed the leather-bound book to Skipper. "Looks like we're missing someone."

"What?"

Claws responded with a light shrug while Skipper studied the open page. Then he gazed at the ceiling of the dome, at the helium balloons floating above him.

"All right. We do a roll call," he announced. He waited a moment to ensure he had everyone's attention. Then in a loud voice, he repeated his command. "Roll call, everyone. I'm going to call out your names in the exact order that you registered for the conference. When you hear your name, raise your hand and say *here."*

He drew a pen from his shirt pocket. "Okay, first up. Eve Noon."

Eve gave a sideways glance at Finch. Should she answer?

"Eve Noon," Skipper bellowed.

She raised her hand. "Here."

"Don't ever make me ask you twice." The mask did nothing to hide the venom in his voice. Skipper narrowed his eyes and stared at her. "Understand?"

"Yes," she said.

"Good." He made a checkmark on the register. "And keep your hand up. Next, Will Finch."

Finch raised his hand. "Here."

Skipper's pen checked the register again. "Keep your hand up," he said. "Everyone, when I call your name, keep your hand up until we're done."

Skipper continued the roll call until he reached the twenty-third name on the list. "Brittany Swank."

No one spoke.

Skipper surveyed the hands still aloft in the air. "Brittany Swank," he repeated.

Nothing.

"Anyone know where Brittany Swank is?"

When no one spoke, Skipper crossed the floor to Eve. "I know you're the conference organizer. Do you know Brittany Swank?"

Caught off guard, Eve had to think. Brittany had registered for the conference on Friday morning. As Roland Clapp had said, later-comers are better than no-shows. She drew a long breath. "Yes."

"Did you see her here this evening?"

Again, Eve hesitated. Brittany Swank was a media branding guru. Known as the Queen of the Scene she'd successfully guided three brand launches during the pandemic. When Eve spoke to Brittany at the kickoff meet-and-greet she'd smiled with the look of a cat about to pounce. "There are at least three companies here courting me," she'd whispered. "I'm so glad you let me join in late." Eve replied with a coy laugh, "Three in one night? Brit, I didn't know you had it in you."

That was around nine o'clock. But she hadn't seen Brittany since. If she'd slipped away, it would be better for Brittany if Skipper thought she'd been gone all night. Maybe Brittany was already in Mendocino and had contacted the police. If she had, it wouldn't be long before the FBI took charge. She shook her head with a feeling of despair. *Too many ifs.*

"No." Eve returned Skipper's intense stare. "Definitely not."

"Anyone else seen her?"

Too terrified to reply, most people shrugged off the question. Five or six muttered an oblique "No."

Skipper drew his shoulders up. Somehow he appeared to grow two inches taller. "All right. *Claws.*"

Claws stood at the ready, then took a step toward Skipper.

"Brittany Swank checked into the Redwood cabin yesterday afternoon. Flush her out. If she's not there, hunt her down. In any case, do *not* come back here empty-handed. Got it?"

The order was issued as a do-or-die command. Loud enough for everyone to hear — and to understand the consequences should anyone else try to escape.

"Copy that." Claws cradled the handguard of his AR-15 in the crook of his left elbow and made his way out the door to the lobby where he slipped into the night.

Finch watched the unfolding drama and realized their tight-knit battle plans had unraveled. Or at least dropped a stitch. He pondered the odds. With Claws tracking down Brittany, and Jasper in the kitchen minding the staff, that left two bandits on the floor. Skipper and Dogboy. How to distract them — and give Eve a chance to escape?

CHAPTER FOUR

EARLIER THAT NIGHT, Brittany Swank felt a shiver of anticipation as she walked from the opening night reception in the Rotunda back to the Redwood cabin.

She'd just arranged a private consultation with Jeff Sconce of Tite-Flite Digital for Saturday morning at ten. To be followed by lunch with Barry "Bigman" Bigalow, the CEO at Profound Sounds, and finally, a chin-wag with her old colleague Nancy Greenlaw who last month launched Media$$, a "bespoke service" (as she called it) targeting media compensation management.

So instead of clinking champagne glasses with her new best friends in the Rotunda, a little after ten PM, Brittany decided to head back to the Redwood cabin to review her notes and presentation slides. She had to be in top form tomorrow and she knew it. First, she set out her clothes for the morning, then sat at the cabin table and opened her laptop. The one thing more important than her Elie Tahari cashmere midi-dress and the matching jacquard jacket was a crystal clear mind. She worked for about three hours, then at one-thirty, she closed her laptop and stood at the sliding door that looked onto the forest. She could still feel shivers of expectation riffing over her skin. Time for some fresh air, she decided.

She tugged on her fleece jacket and San Francisco Giants baseball cap, slipped open the glass door, and stepped onto the tiny concrete deck that looked onto the forest. Are there bears out here? Mountain lions? She let out a sigh. *Duh, course, there are.* You may be a city girl, but you're not a tenderfoot.

She was about to step off the pad and round the corner onto the trail that led back to the resort when she heard a whimper coming from someone heading toward the main office. She pressed her head against the wood siding of the cabin and watched two men in camo gear lead a couple along the path. *My God.* Barry Bigelow, and his girlfriend. Ainsley, that was her name. Brittany held a hand to her mouth to block a cry of shock. One of their captors pushed Ainsley along by her fore-arm and she let out another whimper. *What the hell?*

Brittany watched them march along the trail until they rounded the corner up to the parking lot. Then she saw another couple, Vic and Jenny Wexler — the husband-and-wife duo who owned WMD: Wexler Media Dimensions — led from the front door of the Beechwood by another pair of militiamen. On an impulse, she took one step onto the trail and was about to confront them. But Jenny caught her eye. The slight shake of Jenny's head warned Brittany away. She slipped back behind the corner of the Redwood before the two men could see her.

What the hell?

Brittany zipped her fleece up to her chin and watched the

Wexlers disappear as they reached the top of the trail and turned toward the parking lot. At once reality struck her. The delegates to the conference were being abducted cabin by cabin. She drew a deep breath and understood in an instant: she had to escape. Where? How?

Knowing she had to dart in and out of the Redwood before she was abducted, she prepared a mental list of supplies. First, grab your meds. Then your phone. Your car keys. A water bottle. She ran over the list again and again until she felt certain of her next move. Yes, and shove it all in your day pack. Then she saw a pair of men return from the lodge and approach her cabin.

My God, I'm next.

She stood stock-still on the concrete deck. Then she heard the pounding at the front door. A pause, then a loud bang. Someone called into the cabin, "Wildfire. You got to evacuate. Right now!" Then more concussive hammering at the door. Finally, she heard someone toying with the lock. A moment later, both men stepped inside the cottage.

Brittany scanned the ground behind her, stepped off the patio, and slipped past the ferns and salal and into the woods. She wedged her body behind a fir tree and peered around the tree trunk. One of the men flicked on the overhead lights inside her cottage. They checked the bathroom and stood a moment talking next to her bed. Then they swept her car keys, phone, and laptop into a bag and walked outside. She watched them march along the trail to the next cabin, the one occupied by Frank Winters and his wife, Jeanine. Again the men hammered at the door. Another cry of "Wildfire!" The cabin lights blinked on and five minutes later Frank and Jeanine Winters were shoved out the door and marched up the trail to the resort.

Brittany held a hand to her mouth. Okay. *Think*. You have no phone, no car. The computer's gone. So get your water bottle, some clothes, whatever — *your meds!* — then you run. No, first you hide, make sure the coast is clear, then slip out to the trail. Check what's happening at the lodge. Make sure of things.

Brittany crept through the sliding glass door into the cottage and dashed over to the mini-fridge. As the door opened, the interior light blinked on and revealed her insulin vials and syringe. Three vials lay side-by-side on the top tack. Two were full and the third, the one she used for her current daily doses, held little more than two or three shots. All told, they provided about a month's supply of her medication — the reserve that she'd learned to tuck away when she was seventeen and barely survived her first insulin crash.

She did a quick assessment. Best to carry one full vial and the partial dose with her and leave the second full vial here. Just in case she had to double back to the resort. She nodded to herself. In an emergency, maybe you can get more in Mendocino. She packed the partial vial and syringe in the leather kit — which her teacher once mistook for a glasses case — and tucked it in her daypack and zipped up the flap. On the off-chance that she lost the pack, she decided to slip the single full vial in the back pocket of her jeans. And just in case she had an insulin crash, she packed up some of her favorite low-sugar carbs: a banana, a bunch of grapes, and a baggie of raisins.

She quickly scanned the rest of the fridge. Two bottles of

water, one orange juice, two small bags of mixed nuts, and two cracker packets. In the crisper, she found a ham sandwich wrapped in a plastic triangle pack. Could she take them all? In her day pack maybe. But the clock is ticking, girl. Next to the bathroom door lay her hiking boots. She tugged them on and loaded all the food, water, and juice into her pack. As she imagined hiking through the forest in the dark, she remembered a tiny LED penlight — "f-ing useless," she complained — and shoved it into the front pocket of her fleece jacket. She glanced around the room. What more? *Nothing!* she screamed to herself. Go— *run* — go!

One, two, three, four steps swept her back through the sliding door. She skipped over the concrete deck and into the midnight wilderness of the forest.

Bears, mountain lions, rattlesnakes be damned, she told herself. *You can do this.*

CHAPTER FIVE

BRITTANY FORCED HERSELF to hide in the woods until the last cabin had been cleared. She watched as Eve Noon and Will Finch were escorted along the trail to the resort. Eve, her new friend and ally in navigating the digital media world in the Bay Area. Eve, the one (the only) person who helped win Brittany's first major corporate branding contract.

And now this. Which was what, exactly? Pairs of commandos marched all the conference delegates up to the Rotunda in the dark of night. Brittany waited another twenty minutes to ensure she could walk undetected toward the resort. She hunched behind a cluster of salal shrubs behind the rear of the geodesic dome. To her left the resort's backyard reached into the forest. Not far off stood the wire chicken pen which housed Roland Clapp's prized Mystic Marans hens. "Egg layers, every one of them," Roland had boasted to her that afternoon. On her right, a two-story A-frame seemed to hide in the shadows. The building looked like staff housing, or perhaps it provided overflow guest accommodation. Impossible to tell. Between the back of the lodge and the A-frame stood a small concrete building that served as a food locker for dry goods. A fan slowly rotated inside a steel grill at the top of the locker.

Through the ground-level hexagram windows of the Rotunda, she could see the hostages slumped in a circle on the floor of the dome. A circle of doom, she told herself. Everyone hunched over. Some covered their faces, a few in tears. The commandos — is that what they're called? — towered over them, billy clubs clutched in their fists, rifles strapped across their shoulders.

She pinched her lips together until she felt her teeth bite into her lips. What to do? Then it dawned on her. It wouldn't be long before someone discovered that she'd evaded the roundup. Okay, back to Plan A. Slip behind the A-frame and cross the gravel road that leads down to the front gate. From there make your way down to Big River and out to Mendocino.

She took another moment to count the men. How to tell one from another? They looked like clones. Robots pacing restlessly, some in circles, others treading along an imaginary path that crossed the diameter of the dome. All of them dressed in military camouflage. Cammies, Jonny called them.

She recalled their evenings together in their apartment in Noe Valley. Jonny positioned his cammies for action on the kitchen table. As the battle began he knocked them over, one by one, flicking them with a fingernail. "Unh. Unh," he moaned to suggest their near painless death as they collapsed on his dreamworld battlefield. She never understood it. What kind of crazy society trains little boys to wage war in the family kitchen?

And what would Jonny think if he could see her now? The question defined everything worth living for. She felt an invisible force cross the broken ground from the dome to her hiding place in the salal. Her throat tightened and she gasped for air. No matter what lay ahead, she would survive and make her way back to her son before the weekend was over. Before Jonny realized anything was amiss. Thank God her sister was at home with him. Would Jackie know what to do if something serious happened?

She watched as the men crisscrossed the center of the room. One thumped the business end of his truncheon into the palm of his hand in a steady beat as he marched past the huddled figure of Roland Clapp and over to Eve Noon and Will Finch. He leaned forward and spoke to Eve. A message that inspired a slight shrug from Eve's shoulders. Was he asking Eve about her?

Brittany's heart jumped a beat when one of the cammies marched through the passageway into the resort reception hall. Had he been sent to track her down? Yes, she felt sure of that. She checked her watch — 3:10 AM — then rose from her knees and took a step backward. Another. She slipped behind the trunk of a fir tree and into the cool moon shadows. *Moon shadow, moon shadow,* she hummed to herself.

She found a narrow track through the woods that led around the A-frame building and over a cedar chip path to the driveway where all the conference delegates had parked their rental cars in the lot that faced the broad front deck of the resort. She stepped onto the gravel driveway. When she heard the stones squeak under her hiking boots she paused and lifted her weight onto her toes. All those years spent in ballet class. Now it counted for something as she floated over the crushed rocks and into the forest.

She slipped behind another tree and glanced back at the lodge entrance. The door swung open. She drew a breath and dipped her head behind the tree trunk. She waited as she heard the cammie's feet crunch across the gravel and fade into the distance as he marched down the trail to the resort cabins. She guessed that he'd head back to her cottage. That would give her five minutes to flee in the opposite direction.

She didn't hesitate. She pushed her way through the waist-high salal and fern shrubs, walking parallel to the resort drive-way. If she could flag down a car coming into the resort, then she could use the driver's phone to call 911. Or not. She knew the resort was well off the grid and wondered how many miles she'd have to go to find the range of a cell tower.

As she walked further into the forest her eyes adjusted to the gray shadows cast by the moonlight slanting through the treetops. She drew the penlight from her pocket and clicked it on. "Almost useless," she muttered and cast the thin light across the ground underfoot. Although she could barely make out the knots of the tree roots that twisted up through the dirt path, she pressed on. An hour passed. "Keep going," she muttered and scanned a slope running at a gentle angle on the right. At the bottom of the dip, she detected a shelter under the crooked limbs of a tree blown down in one of the many storms that thrashed the west coast every winter. She stepped off the path and inched along a bank of loose shale. A slip, a slide, and down she went, both feet flying out from under her. Her hands braced to break her fall. The impact was immediate. She fell flat on her buttocks and felt the vial of insulin crunch in her back pocket.

"Fuck!"

She slapped her right hand over her mouth to choke down the pain ripping through her butt. Now what? She drew a deep breath and tried to adjust her backpack. Her thumb hooked one strap over her shoulder. All right. Okay. Now can you sit up? Yes. Her right hand reached into her back pocket and drew out the broken vial of insulin. The medical label held the shattered glass in place but the clear insulin seeped into the ground. "No, no, no," she whimpered.

Her fingers swept over her eyes and she stared into the forest. Beside her, she saw dozens of tree branches, their limbs still holding wisps of foliage. On the ground lay dried leaves, gnarled bark, and patches of thin mulch.

"All right, *enough*. This is where you sleep. Then decide what to do in the morning." She curled her legs up to her waist and drew in a long breath. The wet stink of urine and feces filled her nostrils. What is this place? A bear den?

Let it go, she whispered to herself. Just let it go. Just sleep.

CHAPTER SIX

FINCH RAN A finger over the steri-strips on his forehead. Eve had done a good job of staunching the bleeding, but the bruise welling under the cut made him wince. "A goose egg," his father had called it when Finch failed to catch the fly ball that smacked into his head during his first year playing Little League baseball.

Not the time to reminisce, he chided himself. Better to focus on Eve. Get her moving. He glanced at the digital clock bolted to the wall above the door leading back to the reception hall. 4:20 AM. He studied the two bandits whispering to one another in the center of the Rotunda. Skipper leaned next to Dogboy's ear, engaged in a long explanation of some kind. Tactics, probably. Over an hour had passed since Claws had been dispatched to reel in Brittany Swank. With Jasper assigned to the kitchen, Finch knew that his abductors were vulnerable. He could read the anxiety in Skipper's constant wavering from foot to foot. They had a new problem to solve. One they never anticipated. Better to strike now, he decided, before Claws returned with Brittany in tow.

Finch lifted a hand in the air. "Hey Skipper," he muttered.

Skipper turned in Finch's direction. "What?"

"Gotta use the can."

"Me too." Frank Winters called from the opposite side of the room.

"And me," Jenny Wexler added. "Like, so bad."

"We're all gonna need it," Finch said in a plaintive voice.

Skipper shook his head, a despondent shrug revealed his misgivings. He knew everyone had to piss. Let them stew in their own juices, or let them relieve themselves? No, not for two more days. He turned back to Dogboy, swore under his breath, and made his decision.

"All right. Women first." He swung around to Jenny and pointed two fingers at Dogboy. "You go with him."

"With him?" Jenny Wexler's voice blistered with disgust. "No way. Get the girl."

Through the mask, Finch could see Skipper's eyes narrowing. He strode over to Jenny and threatened her with his club. "What makes you so fucking special?" His voice climbed a wall of anger. "All of you here. What do you think this is about?" He strode around in a wide circle as he spoke. "Your fat fucking wallets. Your Teslas and yachts. You're lucky to still be alive!" He screamed. "Do you *not* get that?"

He stared at Jenny as he thumped the truncheon in his fist. *Whump. Whump.* "Listen, bitch. Hit the can with Dogboy or pee in your panties. Which is it?"

Jenny cast her eyes to the far door. Everyone waited for her to respond. The silence seemed to sink through the air. She lifted her head and tipped her chin toward Dogboy. "Him."

Skipper nodded once, then turned to the woman squatting next to the hall exit. Barry Bigalow's girlfriend.

"Me?" She pointed at her chest.

"Yeah. What's your name, honey?"

Her face flushed and she averted her eyes. "Ainsley."

"Ainsley. You and Jenny, go with Dogboy."

The two women traded a tentative look and rose to their feet. As Dogboy crossed the floor toward the hallway entrance, they trailed behind him, heads bowed, arms crossed over their chests. A few minutes later they returned to the Rotunda and Dogboy escorted another pair of women to the toilets. The rotation continued for another twenty minutes.

When Eve returned from her round, she hunched next to Finch and whispered next to his ear. "I'm ready."

He nodded and mouthed a silent reply. "After I get back." With his hands buried in his lap, a finger pointed toward the crash door.

She blinked once to acknowledge that when his turn for the toilet came around he'd prompt a diversion. Her chance to slip through the exit and make a run for it.

Dogboy led Finch and Jeff Sconce into the men's room and pointed to the row of four urinals under the opaque windows. They were the last two men in the rotation.

"Get on with it," Dogboy muttered in a caustic voice that revealed his distaste for this particular mission.

Under the balaclava, Finch could see his blue eyes dilate as the fluorescent lights faltered and blinked in a random sequence. On his left hand, he bore a military tattoo. A shield struck by twin lightning bolts. He stood five-ten or -eleven. When he saw Finch hesitating, he tipped his head to the first urinal. "I said, on with it, Finch."

So Dogboy knows your name. His lips turned down in a sneer. "Hey, I gotta take a dump." He pressed his hand against the door leading into the furthest stall along the wall.

Dogboy's eyes narrowed. "Make it fast, Finch."

"Look, I got colitis. It takes as long as it takes, okay?"

Dogboy let out a curse as Finch stepped into the stall and slid the lock bar into the latch. He unbuckled his belt, dropped his pants, and sat on the toilet seat. As he urinated, he slid the box of wooden matches from the watch pocket of his jeans. He studied the logo on the small box, amused that his keepsake would now become the device to free Eve from the terrorists' grasp. He slipped two sticks from the small box and set them on top of the toilet paper dispenser. Next, he drew six more matches halfway out of the box so that the match heads were exposed. He took a moment to assess the improvised fuse, then jammed it into the middle of the toilet paper spool.

"Hurry up, Finch. Me and your pal here are waiting on you."

"Give me another minute. As I said, this isn't easy," Finch whined as he pulled his pants back up, and zipped his fly. He took the two matches from the top of the toilet paper rack and pressed them tightly together. Then he flushed the toilet. As the sound of gushing water filled the bowl, he struck both matches along the zipper of his jeans. The matches flared to life. He held them under the six matchheads protruding from the box. They burst into flame which spread along the wood sticks and into the toilet paper spool.

He released the lock and stepped through the stall door, then closed it behind him. He waved an open hand under his nostrils. "Stinkbomb," he muttered with a look of regret. "Part of my condition. It ain't pretty," he added and swung a hand toward the exit as if to usher them through the door.

Dogboy's lips curled into a snarl and he pinched his nostrils between his thumb and forefinger and led the way out of the men's room. As Finch trailed behind Dogboy and Jeff Sconce he heard the toilet paper ignite. *Whoof.* He offered Dogboy an apologetic shrug as they left the lobby and sauntered back into the Rotunda.

Assured that the distraction was in play, he hunkered down on the floor beside Eve. He wondered how long it would take for the resort alarm system to sound. Two minutes? Three? After five minutes passed in silence he glanced at her and shrugged. "Sorry," he whispered. "I thought — "

The shriek of the fire siren cut through the Rotunda. At first, everyone froze. Then an air of panic ignited the room and everyone struggled to stand up — their legs cramped from hours of sitting on the wood floor — and teetered toward the corridor that led to the reception hall.

"Fire!" Finch screamed and a chorus of terrified shrieks echoed through the hall as the hostages lurched forward. He turned to Eve.

She didn't hesitate. She grabbed her socks and shoes in one hand then eased the crash door open with her hip. Three quick steps and she stood outside the Rotunda. She guided the door back into place. It emitted a gentle click as the latch slipped into the strike plate. She swung around, spotted the food locker, and thirty feet beyond it, the A-frame. She slipped on her shoes, tucked her socks into her pocket, and ran past the buildings into the forest.

CHAPTER SEVEN

CLAWS CHECKED HIS watch before he entered the Redwood cottage. Middle of Saturday night and here he was on the prowl. A feeling of nervous contempt welled through his belly. Nervous because if he found Brittany Swank cowering under the bed or in a closet, he worried that he might not be able to contain his anger. Contempt because she was a woman. Simple as that. Like most of the militia fighters he'd encountered, he knew that women just didn't rank. But you had to protect them because they were necessary. A few of them — very few — knew how to treat you right. A woman like Jasper. She was one of the very few. She loved him like a bear. No fooling around with her. She gave as much as she took, and she took a helluva lot. He knew he'd never marry, but in another world — in another life maybe — Jasper would be his wife.

Next to the front door inside the cottage, he found two pairs of dress shoes, but no loafers. No running shoes. Below the bathroom mirror, he found an array of cosmetics lined in a row, labels facing out. Then he rifled through her suitcase and a fancy leather briefcase. None of it was total-on girly, the way he expected. No sign of her wallet. No jacket or jeans in the closet. He checked the refrigerator. On the top rack, he found a vial of medication with a label he couldn't read or make sense of. Otherwise, except for a six-pack of beer and two mini bottles of wine, the fridge stood empty. Everything else had been liberated. *Liberated,* Dogboy's favorite word for his compulsive petty thieving. Claws shrugged. "Liberated, it is then," he mumbled as he peeled two cans of beer from the plastic retainer and slipped them into his shoulder pack.

Convinced that Brittany Swank had cottoned onto their operation, Claws sat on the bed and stared at the patio door. His head nodded slightly as he calculated the possibilities. Yup, that's where she'd make her break. Out the side door. Then up the path to the Rotunda, along the road back to Mendocino? Thirty miles. Not easy for anyone let alone a single chick hooked on a bunch of facial creams. He checked his watch again. Maybe she had a two-hour lead on him. At best, she'd cover five miles. Okay then, game on.

As he walked back to the Rotunda he adjusted his gear and began to jog along the trail to the gravel road that led back to Mendocino. After a mile, he turned right onto the service road, a narrow track with two ruts pounded down by years of tires rolling over the dirt and weeds.

At the end of the service road stood three identical buildings. Their doors were locked, the windows protected by racks of steel bars. One building was equipped with tools, saws, and work benches. The middle building looked like an auto body shop. The third housed an old-time tractor probably used to clear the deadfall when winter storms blew the big trees across the road.

The Hummer was parked behind the middle of three maintenance buildings. He pulled the balaclava from his face and looped it around his belt. He hated the damn things. His face felt the constant prickle of the material needling his skin. But Skipper insisted on it whenever they were in the lodge. Now that he'd cut free from the unit and entered his natural element on his own, Claws didn't have to follow any of Skipper's orders but one. *"Hunt her down."*

He plucked the ignition fob from the sun visor and climbed into the driver's seat. He decided to drive without headlamps. No need to alert her as he closed the gap. He fired the ignition and let the Hummer advance at an idle up to the main road, where he turned right and drove west toward Mendocino.

Fifteen miles along the roadway he coasted to a stop, then made a U-turn on a narrow shoulder and turned the Hummer around. He killed the ignition and stared into the darkness. Think about it, he told himself. No way she could cover that distance in two hours. Not like this. Not in the dark. He opened a can of beer and slugged it back in three pulls. All right. So she must be trying to make her way through the bush. Pretty stupid. Too stupid for her own good.

He cranked down the window, tossed the beer can past the salal, and opened the second beer. After a moment he started the engine. He noted the miles on the odometer, notched the Hummer into first gear, and coasted along the road back toward the lodge.

CHAPTER EIGHT

AS A TEENAGER, Eve Noon had medalled every year in her school district's long-distance footraces. In her senior year, she placed seventh in California State 10K championships. Her best time was 1:00:21. Twenty-one seconds above one hour. Since then she'd maintained a steady running discipline. "It's my meditation," she told Will Finch shortly after they'd met — when they collaborated to solve Gianna Whitelaw's murder. At the time Finch worked as a crime reporter investigating a Bitcoin scandal, and Eve freelanced as a private eye after winning an out-of-court case against the San Francisco Police Department. The settlement came at a cost to her, too. She'd been dismissed from the SFPD after four years of service as a beat cop. As a condition of the generous payout, she signed an NDA which blocked her from revealing the harassment she'd endured on the force. The enforced silence never sat well with her.

Over the years, Finch occasionally joined her on her jogs around the city or through the trails above the Berkeley Hills.

However, he never devoted himself to the transcendent experience of running the way Eve did.

But today she knew that her run had nothing to do with sports or epiphanies. It was about survival. She'd covered about five miles along the winding road toward the village of Mendocino when she heard the thrum of a vehicle approaching from the west. She paused to consider the possibilities. Had Brittany made it into town already? Had she somehow — in the middle of the night — convinced the police to investigate a hostage-taking somewhere below Snow Mountain? She spat a line of spittle onto the gravel. Not likely. Her years working at the San Francisco Police Department had drilled a chronic cynicism into her bones.

In the distance, the sound of the approaching car submerged her questions under the low throbbing of a heavy engine.

As the vehicle approached, she stepped into the cover offered by the forest shadows. An aging redwood tree provided a wide screen to conceal her body. She pressed her belly against the dry bark and eased her head around the tree trunk to watch the road. It took another thirty seconds for the car to crawl into view. A Hummer coasting along in low gear. At the wheel, she could make out one of her captors swiveling his head from side to side. No mask. His face, illuminated by the dashboard light, revealed a glimpse of his wide, flat nose. A three-day scruff of beard. Black, tousled hair. His lips fixed in a sneer. When he lifted his hand to drink from a beer can she saw the row of sheared fingers gripping the aluminum sleeve.

"Claws," she murmured.

She checked her watch. Not long ago Skipper had ordered Claws to capture Brittany. And he was still looking. His head shifted to the right. Ugly bastard, she thought, then issued herself a warning. *Do not mess with him.*

As long as he patrolled the road, she'd be in jeopardy. Time for plan B. Make a beeline through the forest for Big River. Then follow it downstream through the valley to the beach where the river slipped into the Pacific. That would put her just south of Mendocino. Although she hadn't run a marathon in three years, she figured the thirty-mile run along the road into town would take her a little over six hours. Without water, the journey would be impossible. Now that she had to pick her way through the forest, it could take twice as long. With luck, you can be there before dusk. But only if the river is running. Without water, you might not make it at all.

CHAPTER NINE

A LITTLE PAST the twelve-mile mark on his odometer, Claws saw something startle and dash into the forest. He smiled at that.

"All right bitch, get ready."

He paused to consider his situation, then drove back to the maintenance yard, parked behind the middle service building, cut the engine, and put the keys under the sun visor on the driver's side. He strapped his AR-15 over his shoulder and jogged along the short stretch back to the main road. When he reached the lip of the forest, at the point where he'd seen something scramble into the bushes, he drew the SIG Sauer P226 from his holster and paused to assess the way ahead. The 226 was better for close-quarter combat in the bush, he told himself. He drew his flashlight into his left hand and clicked it on. To the right, he spotted a depression in the salal. He stepped forward and pushed his way past the shrubs and waded into the stand of pine trees.

He sniffed the air. Two deep snorts.

"Yo, Brittany. I know you're here, lady. Saw you from the road. Make this easy on the both of us, okay. Just come out now and we'll head back to the lodge together."

He heard something scuttle through bushes to his left. He swung the lamp around and slid his finger against the SIG's trigger guard.

"Like I said, Ma'am. I've got some food and water in the car for you, so let's make this easy. No harm, no foul. All right?"

He waited. Where the hell had she slinked off to? Now the scuttling sounded from somewhere behind him. He turned the lamp and saw the eyes of the bear flash as it charged toward him. One, two, three strides before he could react. He fired two rounds from his pistol. The animal groaned as it barreled ahead. He drew a breath and stumbled backward as the beast raked its claws across his chest.

"Fuck!"

He shot another five rounds point-blank into the bear's massive torso, then Claws lost his balance and crashed onto the ground. He braced himself and rose onto his knees just as the beast flopped forward onto his left front leg. Then his head slumped onto the dirt and he began bawling miserably.

Claws swung the flashlight from side to side to assess the damage. The animal looked huge. Was it a grizzly? He shrugged off the question. Who could tell?

"Jesus in Hell," he muttered when he realized how close he'd come to losing everything. He stood and brushed the dirt from his chest. "Lucky you're wearing a combat vest," he said. An expression from his two years in Afghanistan came to mind. Something Mickey Palance said when they survived a Taliban ambush. "What Fate forgets, sometimes Luck provides."

The bear groaned in a long series of broken whimpers. Claws stepped forward and shook his head with disbelief. He ran a hand over his chest to see if the bear had cut him. His vest was torn open and his Icom two-way radio transceiver totally destroyed. Apart from that, no damage. But without the transceiver, he had no way to contact Skipper.

"You were *this* close," he told the bear. *"This fuckin' close."*

He stood above the animal and studied the wide snout, the long snaggletoothed mouth, the eyes blinking helplessly, as his troubled breathing slipped through its wet, black nostrils. His legs trembled as Claws leveled his pistol at the bear's low forehead. He aimed directly between the brown eyes gazing back at him. He shuddered when he realized how very human they looked. He drew a breath and fired a single round. When the pistol report faded he paused to study the animal for signs of life. Nothing. Claws's lips curled as he was acknowledging the power of the bear. And that this is how all life ends. Man or beast. Your heart stops and your lungs give up that last gasp of air. Then it's just over and out.

There's nothing more, but a whole lot less.

CHAPTER TEN

DESPITE THE CRACKLE of gunfire, neither Brittany nor Eve — both sheltering miles from one another — heard the gunshots from Claws's battle with the bear. The towering trees and the compact density of the forest served as a natural noise suppression device. And the hostages, cowering in the well-insulated lodge, heard little more than their own sobs and whimpers.

As she struggled to find her bearings, Brittany could barely hear the skittering of squirrels and the whispers of birds coming to life around her. The bear den — if that's what it was — hadn't been occupied for a while. At least that's what she told herself when the dawn light illuminated the shallow cavern where she'd rested over the past few hours. A second thought seemed to clutch at her throat. At least a dozen predators might fight her to regain possession of the lair. Mountain lions, wolves, coyotes. Perhaps a pregnant bear returning to her old home to prepare for hibernation. No matter who might step into the ring against her, she knew she'd lose in the first round.

In any case, she understood that she had to move on. Likely one of the cammies was tracking her. Which meant returning to the Redwood cottage was out of the question. Since the broken insulin vial in her back pocket was useless, she had to rely on the vial stored in her backpack. Trouble was, it held only enough insulin for one day, maybe two if she rationed it. At best, that gave her two days to find her way to Mendocino and find a pharmacy.

She checked her watch. Saturday, 6:42. Time to move on. She set a vibrating alarm for 8:00. A reminder to check her glucose monitor. Then she'd reset the alarm for 9:00 and every following hour. Vigilance was essential. She tore open the plastic sleeve of a bag of nuts and chewed on two cashews as she contemplated her next move. First, determine the direction to Big River. The map in the lodge showed that the river was located south of the resort. Which meant if she kept the sun on her left side through the morning she could reach the river by noon. Then all she had to do was follow the shoreline to the oceanfront in Mendocino. As she crushed the nuts between her teeth, she examined the contents of the daypack. She tugged her running shoes from the bottom of the pack, then unlaced her hiking boots, attached them to the two carabiners on the shoulder straps, and slung the pack over her shoulders. After she balanced their weight, she slipped the runners on her feet. Funny. She'd never used a carabiner before. Until now, she thought they were useless appendages. It was Jonny who insisted that she purchase a pack with the carabiners when they visited REI last April.

"It's so cool, Mom. You can use them for mountain climbing."

Mountain climbing. She wiped a tear from her eye and let out a light gasp. Where was he? Her sister Jackie would have put him to bed with a story and cuddled him until he fell asleep. Jackie loved Jonny almost as much as she did.

"Thank God," she whispered and began to pray for her son, her sister, her mother, and her long-lost father.

It took three attempts to adjust the pack straps until she felt comfortable. A flash of pain darted along her back. Her forefinger grasped at the left strap. She winced and made another slight adjustment. It wasn't perfect, but it would do.

She swallowed a gulp of water and decided to drink only when her throat felt parched. She had two bottles of water and one of orange juice. She would drink the diluted juice only when she needed the sugar boost. Her diabetic condition made that a special challenge. One she'd had to navigate since the day of her diagnosis. She was seventeen years old with two girlfriends and a boyfriend who, within two months, all tactfully disappeared from her life. At least she was smart. Smart enough to know she had to make her own way in the world. A good lesson to learn in adolescence.

Her feet found some traction as she clambered up the slope onto level ground. She walked a few paces and then turned to face the dim glow of light cast through the forest by the rising sun. East, she reminded herself. That'll guide your direction until you reach Big River. From there, you turn right and follow the river until you arrive in Mendocino. Thirty miles through the bush. How long would it take? She scanned the trees, the salal, the broken rubble scattered across the hill on her right. As her eyes adjusted to the wilderness, she could make out a thin track ahead. She stepped forward and followed the trail for twenty yards until it faded into the roots of an ancient, desiccated pine that had collapsed into a ditch. She swung around, searching for something, anything that could point out a direction to the river. Nothing. *Nothing.*

"Please Jesus, help me," she whimpered and turned her attention to the pale sky above. She adjusted the shoulder strap and began to repeat the old prayer from her school. The words drilled into her every morning from kindergarten through the day she graduated from Marymount School. The prayer had provided the touchstone she needed to navigate her way through her illness. And now it came to her again. *Hail Mary full of grace, the Lord is with thee, blessed art thou amongst women.*

As she recited the incantation she stepped forward through the waist-high scrub. Her right hand batted away the branches and shrubs that slapped her knees and thighs. When her wrist alarm buzzed, she found a clearing and sat on a round slab of granite that rose a foot or two above the ground. She checked her continuous glucose monitor, an electronic marvel the size of a silver dollar, embedded just below her right shoulder. The CGM fed a data stream to an app on her cell phone. She turned on her phone, checked the glucose reading, and let out a puff of air. All good. "Until your cell runs out of juice," she murmured. The phone battery level read 19%. By the end of tomorrow, she'd be lucky to get any readings at all. Without the CGM or any finger prick tests, she'd have no idea if her glucose levels were rising or falling — and she'd have no idea when she'd need another insulin dose. "You'll be flying blind, kiddo," she muttered and shook her head in dismay.

During the pandemic, she'd fallen a step behind the current diabetes management technology. When her new business began to generate more money she intended to purchase an insulin pump that fed a precise dose of insulin into her body based on the readings from her CGM. The pump held a five-day reservoir. Enough to get to Mendocino and back, she figured. "Well, that was then," she wheezed, "and this is now."

She turned the phone off and tucked it into her pocket, sipped some water, and considered the sweep of clouds sailing past the withered trees above her. The drought had taken a heavy toll on them. She could smell their thirst. Everything in the forest looked parched. The scent of tinder-dry kindling rose from the needles and leaves on the forest floor.

She took another sip of water and chastised her laziness. Okay, just get down to Big River, she told herself. She adjusted the pack straps on her shoulders and wobbled as she struggled to regain her balance. She studied the sky again. Now that the sun was up, she felt assured that she could find her way. "There." Her right hand pointed into the forest ahead.

Sixty minutes later her watch began to vibrate. Nine o'clock. Time for her medication check. Then to her left, she spotted a shadow hunched above the ground a little past an opening in the bush. A bear? She held her breath and stood motionless while she studied the dark mass. Heavy. Thick. She became a deer, stock-still, her ears sifting the air for any vibrations. A drizzle of perspiration slipped from her forehead. Was she downwind? Could the beast sniff her out? She put one foot forward. Another. Then stood still to determine if the creature would respond to her movement. Nothing. Reassured, she moved across the ground in a steady, silent gait. She let out a gasp. A laugh. *The beast is a flippin' car.* A broken-down jalopy somehow dropped here in the middle of the forest and left to rust.

She swung around to look for any signs of a road. There had to be some evidence of dirt tracks that led this old-timer into the middle of nowhere. She walked around the vehicle. The rusty remains of the front doors had fallen off and dropped to the ground where they'd partially dissolved into the soil. The car trunk was still in place. Above the lift handle, an oval plaque identified the car: FORD V8. She tried to lift the lid. Rusted shut. She wedged a knee on the bumper and tried again. No way. Except for the FORD V8 shield which rattled loose. She caught it in her right hand.

"Crazy."

She turned it over and over in her fingers, wondering what to do with it. She shrugged off her pack, unzipped the front pouch, and slipped the plaque inside. Her little treasure from the time she was lost in the woods. Jonny would love that. The story about how she got lost in the wilderness, totally on her own, found this rusting old Ford, then made her way home all by herself. A lesson in perseverance. When you don't know what to do, you just keep going.

She pressed a foot against the rear bumper and tested its strength under the weight of her leg. Good. She rested her buttocks on the car trunk, took a sip of water, then swallowed a deep drink in a long swallow. Again she checked her continuous glucose monitor. Time for a dose of insulin. Over the years the needle injection process became a matter of course and she'd become numb to the tiny pin-pricks she'd endured. She prepared the syringe, administered the shot, then carefully packed the needle next to the vial in its case and slipped the kit into her pack.

As she stared into the distance, a thought came to her. The car could only have traveled into the forest on *some* kind of road. And a hundred years ago where were roads built? Along the river valleys. That meant a river flowed somewhere nearby. Big River had to be close. She attuned her ears to the sound of running water. Nothing. But it had to be close.

She hoisted her weight from the Ford, found her bearings again, and trudged forward. She decided to march east a hundred paces. If she found nothing, she'd turn right and walk another hundred paces. Then left. As she walked she was happy to count off the paces. Ten, eleven, twelve. Better than endlessly reciting Hail Marys.

After twenty minutes of walking back and forth, left and right, she felt her chest squeezing with every breath. Here's something new. Something she'd never felt before. She stopped, struggled to keep her balance, then plopped onto a half-dead salal shrub. Her right hand clasped her chest. Fuck. What *is* this? A heart attack? Her lips pursed into a tight funnel and she breathed deeply. In, out. In, out. She counted the breaths and when she hit twenty, she let out a long puff of air. No, not a heart attack. Just panic. Admit it, *you're completely lost.* Just absorb that feeling. *Own it,* then figure out what to do. She struggled to her feet and scanned the forest around her. The abandoned Ford was nowhere in sight. But to her right, the woods appeared to thin out. A shaft of light clipped the shadows into thin bars that opened into … what?

She ran her hand over her face and stepped toward the wedge of daylight. Yes. Dear God, this is the way. *Hail Mary full of grace, the Lord is with thee, blessed art thou amongst women.*

Moments later she stood on the lip of a dry river bed. A bed of sun-baked stones and river rock traversed from one side of the forest to the other. "No wonder you couldn't hear the water," she mumbled. "There isn't any."

The smooth rocks and stones were stacked by the river currents years ago when the waters once flooded with the glacial runoff from Snow Mountain. Again she recalled the wall map in the lodge. Snow Mountain marked the high point in the range to the east. And here lay the ruins of what was once a vibrant rainforest. Stones strewn in heaps that fell away on the downstream side of the river. A large boulder stood in the middle of the passage, twenty feet to the west. She picked her way over to the sunny side of the rock and caressed the surface with her hand. It offered some heat, enough to bring a smile to her lips. She eased off her backpack and rested her back along the smooth, wide face of the granite surface. Once again she examined the CGM reading on her phone (glucose good for now, but only a 12% phone battery reserve), then drew the sandwich package from the backpack and turned it in her hands. Two stickers adorned the clear plastic seal. One read HAM, the other, Courtesy of Big River Resort. A small tear in the seal protruded from the corner. Her front teeth clamped onto the edge and she peeled the plastic away. She spat it onto the riverbed stones at her feet and dumped the sandwich into her lap.

"Oh my God," she whispered after her teeth cut through the bread. "You are so effing delicious!" She took another bite, then drank from the water bottle.

Effing? Listen to yourself, girl. Are you so uptight that you even can't say *fucking* out loud? She raised her chin and let out a cry. *"Fuck! I am so fucking lost!"*

All right. Enough. What if the cammies hear you? By now, they know you escaped. Make no mistake, they're coming for you.

Yes, you're right. She nodded in agreement, put the remains of the sandwich in the container, and slipped it into the backpack. "We'll save you for dinner," she whispered to the sandwich. "After we find a place to sleep. Right? Yes, agreed."

She felt a dull ache in her lower back and washed a Tylenol pill down with some water. Then she slipped the bottle into the webbing on the side of the pack and slipped it over her shoulders. She pushed away from the massive rock and took a step toward the far side of the river bed where the rocks appeared to offer better footing. Along the river bank, she followed a new deer track that led around a bend. Two hours later she paused for another sip of water. After a moment of debate, she ate the banana and tossed the skin onto the rocks.

It was then — as her eyes gauged the distance along the shoreline — that she noticed the shack in the forest.

CHAPTER ELEVEN

EVE PUSHED THROUGH the salal shrubs that filled the space between the stand of birch and fir trees. The sun now stood directly above her. She checked her watch. Noon. Her surname. Her father had told her their name marked the best time of day. A time when everyone was wide awake, looking for a break from work or school, eager to take some nourishment and talk with some friends. "A much better name than Dawn or Dusk," he said with a doubtful chuckle as if he didn't believe it himself. The memory made her laugh. Her name could've been Eve Dusk. Or Eve Midnight. Stripper names.

About ten minutes later, the trees seemed to thin and she detected an opening ahead. Then she saw the space where the river turned in one long curl through the narrow valley.

"Big River," she muttered. "What a joke." She studied the terrain upstream, the bleak dry hills of the coast mountains. The wide bed of river rocks crossed to the far side of the empty creek. She felt the arid heat radiate from the stones up into her face. Was there any water here at all? She stepped over to the middle of the river bed, bent at her waist, and turned a rock upside down. The bottom face was bone dry. Below that sat another dry stone. Below that two more.

"Damn," she muttered and began to walk downstream. Somewhere ahead the water had to sink into a pool. The drought had run on for over ten years but somewhere — *somewhere* — there had to be water.

She plodded onward and when she turned past a gray dirt bank she spotted a large boulder the size of a truck standing in the middle of the creek. When she reached it, she paused to get her bearings again. On the left, a trail ran through the scrub next to a line of birch trees. If she could find a decent path maybe she could begin running again. She wet her lips and started to canter along an uneven deer track. Go slow, she warned herself. Sprain an ankle out here and you're finished.

Twenty minutes later a new surprise startled her. She rubbed a hand over her face and braced her feet on the edge of the narrow path. Above the track stood a shack with two broken windows, a half-hinged door, and a tattered roof canting sideways over a narrow porch. The building had endured a fire that blackened the wood siding and timbers. She climbed the shallow bank onto a ridge that led up to the door. To her left, she spotted a rat trap that held the white bones of its victim. Further along, the remains of a rabbit lay snared in a wire noose.

She paused to consider the abandoned traps. What the hell was this place? She brushed a fly from her face. The sun felt hot on her skin and she held a hand at her forehead to block the sun from her eyes. She walked up to the foot of the porch.

Careful, she told herself. She pitched her voice in a low alto toward the door.

"Hello?"

Nothing.

She stepped onto the porch and felt the floorboards sag underfoot.

"Hey. Anyone here?"

Light, kitty-cat footsteps crossed from the back of the shack toward her. Then Brittany's eyes peered around the door jam.

"Eve? Is that you?"

"My God. Brittany — I can't believe it!"

"Eve. Eve!" She let out a cry and held a hand over her mouth as if she had to block any noise that might give her away.

Brittany held up a hand as Eve began to cross the porch to embrace her friend. "Careful. It's rotten. I broke through just over there." She pointed to a gaping hole in the punky wood on Eve's left. "Fell in up to my knee."

Eve stopped and glanced around the deck. "Is it safe?"

"No, but the inside's better than the outside. Well, almost. Walk along the edge of the wall." She pointed to a few planks that had survived the worst of the fire. "Right there."

Eve set her left foot against the exterior wall and made her way along the edge and through the doorway into the shadows of the cabin. The interior stank of charred wood — the black stench of coal dust. Opposite the door stood a steel wood stove. The chimney stack, fallen away from the roof, slumped against the wall. The scorched remains of a table and two chairs had collapsed on the seared planks that formed the floor. A metal-framed bed sat under the window to the left of the door. Everything else, burnt beyond recognition.

"What is this place?"

A bewildered look crossed Brittany's face. "I think a madman lived here."

"What?"

"Yeah. I call it the Burnt Embers Hotel." She let out a sardonic laugh. "Looks like someone started a fire in the floor" — her hand swung around to the back wall where the blackened floorboards had collapsed into the dirt foundation — "*after* the first fire destroyed the place."

"What do you mean?"

"See for yourself."

Brittany led her to the far wall and pointed to the charred pit in the floor. A jagged opening in the floorboards appeared to be an open grave.

"What the hell?" Eve leaned forward to try to make sense of the seared remains at their feet.

"Tell me that's not a corpse," Brittany whispered as if a ghost had slipped behind them. "Burnt to a crisp."

Eve shook her head in disbelief. Then she saw what looked like a bracelet clinging to the blackened ulna and radius bones of a human wrist.

"You see that?"

"I think it's a medical bracelet." Brittany held up her left wrist. "Like mine."

"I think you're right."

"So ... what should we do about him — or her?"

"Right now? Nothing." Eve took a backward step and ran

her hand over her mouth. Her tongue felt thick and dry. She glanced around the walls of the shack and noticed Brittany's backpack slumped under the second window. "Do you have any water?"

Brittany blinked. "A little. You didn't bring any?"

She shook her head. "I had to run."

"What about Will?"

She glanced away. "No. They're holding everyone captive in the Rotunda."

Brittany's eyes swept across the floor as she tried to make sense of their situation. "What about the cammies? Did they follow you?"

"Who?"

"The soldiers."

"They're not soldiers. They're terrorists."

"What do they want?"

They want to kill us. But she swallowed the words and ran her tongue over her lips and pointed to the backpack. "Brit, I really need a drink."

"Yeah. Of course." Wary of stepping through the floor again, she tiptoed to her pack, drew out one of the water bottles, and passed it to Eve. "There's only this and one more. And a bottle of orange juice." She narrowed her eyes with a look of determination. "But I have to save that."

Eve turned the bottle cap and took a sip of water. "Thanks." She took another pull, deeper this time, and passed the bottle back to her friend. "You're saving the juice?"

"In case I need it." She crossed her arms and clutched the bottle to her chest. Her lips fluttered as if she had to block herself from revealing a secret. Then she realized she had to let it out.

"Look." Her chin notched to one side. "I'm diabetic. Type one," she added. "That's why I stopped here when I found this place. At first, I thought I could just follow the river down to Mendocino and get more insulin. Now I know I can't go on. Last night I fell and broke a backup insulin vial. I've got a tenth of a vial left. After today …" Her voice trailed off as her wrist swung toward the backpack. "When it runs out, I've got some raisins and grapes I brought with me. And some diluted juice."

"That's enough to keep you going?"

"Until I zone out." Her hand washed over her face. "It's called a crash. Look, I have to go back to the resort. I left some insulin there, thinking" — she shook her head in dismay — "Well … not thinking straight as it turns out."

Eve responded with a half-smile. "What about food?"

"I've got what's left of a sandwich. A pack of nuts and some fruit." A frown crossed her lips. "But I might need that too."

"It's all about blood-sugar balance, right?"

"Something like that." She shook her head as if she didn't want to discuss what might happen if she crashed. "What about the cammies?"

"The cammies?" She accepted the word as a link to Brittany's world. "Yeah, well. There are four of them. They sent one to look for you. He drove up the road in a Hummer, then doubled back. That's when I saw him. If we're lucky, he didn't see me. Which gives us an advantage."

"What do you mean?"

"He doesn't know it's two against one."

She glanced away, unsure where this was heading. "So, then … what next?"

"My guess is he'll do exactly what we did. Make his way to the river and follow it downstream."

"Until he gets here, you mean."

"Probably." Eve scanned the room, looking for anything that could help them. Weapons. A tarnished kettle sat on the stovetop. Two metal coffee cups lay upside down next to the remains of the scorched table. The steel bed springs were still intact. *The bed frame.* If she could dismantle the rails, they'd possess four spears — two long, two short.

"Look, let's face facts. There's at least one cammie looking for us. He could be here" — she pointed to the open door — "in two minutes. Or two hours. Certainly before dark."

Brittany let out a light gasp. "Two…"

"Either way, we have to be ready to fight." She studied Brittany's face and recognized the fear welling in her eyes. "But we get to pick our ground."

"Our ground? *What* ground?"

The depth of Brittany's inertia sank through Eve's stomach. What help could she possibly offer? "Look. We can try to lure him inside here. Maybe he'll crash through the porch, too. Like you did. Then we go at him. I'm going to try and take the bed apart. Use the steel struts from the frame."

"Maybe…" Her head swiveled from side to side. "Eve, maybe we should try talking to him. Look, that's what we're *good* at. Both of us."

Eve stepped forward and grasped Brittany's hands. "Brittany, listen to me. They've already beaten some of the men. They think they're starting some kind of revolution." She took a moment to look into her eyes. "They have clubs, semi-automatic pistols, AR-15s. If we don't fight back, they're going to kill us."

Brittany began to choke down gulps of air. "My God. Oh, my God — help us," she panted, eyes blinking shut. Then she pulled her hands from Eve's fingers and wrapped her arms around Eve's shoulders. After a moment she recovered. "Eve, I was never a cop like you. I've never been in a fight in my life. *I don't know how.*"

"Like I said. We have no choice. We have to fight." Eve withdrew from the embrace and stared into her eyes again. "Once it starts, believe me, you'll know what to do. You kick his balls in. You scratch his eyes. Punch his throat. Bite his nose and ears." She pinched her lips together with a look of determination. "But right now, we can get ready and wait inside. Or we can prepare for him outside. Somewhere in the woods."

"No. Definitely not outside. Didn't you see the traps?"

A puzzled look crossed her face. "You mean the rat trap?"

"There's like six of them. And not just for rats. Big traps. Huge ones covered up in leaves and branches. After I saw one, I started looking. There's all kinds of them." She threw her hands into the air. "I'm telling you, a crazy guy lived here. So crazy he killed someone, then set his own place on fire."

Eve walked to the window and stared down the gentle slope to the riverbed. Brittany was right. None of the trees had been scorched. Just the cabin itself. Despite the forest fires raging through California and up through Canada, the woods along Big River had been spared. So far.

"Yeah. You're right." Now she could make out a depression in the ground just past the porch. Was it one of the traps?

"You mean that he burned down this place?"

"I mean the traps. I think I see one."

"You're lucky you didn't step in it."

"Guess I am." Eve chuckled, a bleak acknowledgment that she'd dodged a major hazard. Then she turned her attention to the steel bed frame. She knelt at the headboard and examined the construction. The joints were made with slotted knobs and wing nuts. Good. No tools required to disassemble it. She tried to turn a wing nut. "Brit, do you have a shirt or something in your pack? Something I can wrap around this nut while I loosen it."

She rummaged through the pack for a moment. "I brought extra socks. Will that do?"

"Maybe." Eve bunched a sock between her thumb and forefinger and tried to turn one of the wing nuts. "Got it." After a few minutes, she loosened all the head and foot rails from the cross bars. Then she detached the coil springs and the bed frame lay in pieces on the floor. She passed a long rail to her friend. "Try this."

Brittany lifted the steel rail in both hands. She tested its weight and swung it through the air like a broad sword.

"Try using it like a spear." She took the other long rail in her hands to demonstrate. "Go for his belly. Big target first. When he stumbles, smash him across his head."

"Across his head?" She looked doubtful.

"Yeah. If you injure his belly first, he'll drop his hands." Eve tightened her grip on the steel, then swung the rail like a baseball bat. "Then hit him as hard you can."

CHAPTER TWELVE

BRITTANY COULD NOT be budged from the cabin. Rather than argue the point, Eve suggested that maybe, just maybe, they'd have a tactical advantage if Brittany held her ground inside and lured Claws up onto the porch. If Eve hid outside, she could attack him from behind.

The forest on the east side of the shack, a stand of towering redwood trees, offered the perfect blind where she could wait for Claws. She scanned the ground and picked her way over to a massive tree and leaned on the trunk. Her head inched forward as she surveyed the riverbed on her right. Unless Claws possessed uncanny stealth, she'd hear his feet clattering along the stones as he approached the cabin.

Above all, she had to avoid the traps planted around the cabin like land mines. The snares were covered with thin layers of dirt, leaves, withered twigs, branches that had died during the drought, and a dusting of ashes and cinders from the house fire. Brittany had it right. A crazy man had once lived here. A murderer. An arsonist. Someone so starved for fish and game that he'd resorted to devouring rats, rabbits, and squirrels. Who knew what else?

Brittany had offered Eve a mini-bag of nuts along with the few ounces of water that remained in one of her water bottles. While she waited, Eve crushed a few nuts between her teeth until they formed a paste which she slipped onto her tongue. So good. She sealed the remaining nuts in the baggie and shoved it into her jeans pocket. Save it for breakfast, she told herself. She washed the food down with a mouthful of water, capped the bottle, and set it next to the steel bed rail at her feet.

"Okay. You're ready," she murmured and drew a taut breath. Recalling the tension she felt as she climbed into the foot blocks at the start of the 100-meter dash, she nodded to herself. You always feel this way at first. But once the starting gun fires, the other feeling comes. The adrenaline. The drive to win.

She checked her watch. 5:23. The fall equinox had passed last week, so about another hour until sunset. She thought her chances against Claws might improve in the dark. If he didn't know she was waiting for him, she'd have the element of surprise. In the dark, her advantage would be doubled.

Moments later she heard the click-clack of stones chinking together. Soft at first. Perhaps a crow had dropped some nuts onto the river rocks. She listened to the sounds of the trees swaying in the wind, the sound of her heart thrumming. *There.* Another crack sounded when a heavy rock turned under a boot heel. She grasped the bed frame rail in both hands and curled her fingers around the steel to test the weight.

She turned toward the shack and tossed a few pebbles onto

the porch. Their signal. Brittany had insisted that Eve warn her when she heard the cammie approach. Eve didn't think it was smart. Especially if Brittany panicked. Who knew how Claws might react if she screamed? He could march up the slope, throw her on the floor, and take her. Or simply unload a magazine of .223 Remington bullets through the front of the cabin. A blast from a modified AR-15 would likely rip through the charred walls and kill or maim her. That would be the easiest way for Claws to put her down, Eve mumbled to herself. But then, who knew what kind of passions drove a man like him? A disabled mercenary paid to kill innocent women.

But Brittany didn't react to the sound of the pebbles tripping across the scorched deck. Maybe she'd bottled up her fear. Maybe she could muster the guts to see this through.

When Eve caught her first glimpse of him, she turned her head away. *This is it. It's really gonna happen.* But not yet. Not til you say so. She nodded her head. You have control, so *look* at him. See what he's got. Find the spot to plunge the rail into his back. Go for his spine. Maybe the kidneys.

He edged up the rising ground from the far side of the river — on the north bank, opposite the route Eve had taken to the shack. His grim, unshaven face bore a look of stony determination. He slipped the handguard of his AR-15 into his left hand and nudged the rifle butt against his right shoulder. Look at this, she whispered to herself. A bump stock retro-fitted to the rifle, making it a fully automatic military-grade weapon. *These creeps mean business.*

He took his time to approach the porch, his feet grazing the ground at a slow, stealthy pace. An expression of wariness settled on his face. He halted and began to circle behind the shack. When he disappeared from her line of sight, Eve turned her attention to the front door and windows. She couldn't hear any noise from Brittany. Was she still cowering next to the wood stove? Eve had told her that the steel box might screen her from a direct hit. But she didn't mention the hazard from stray bullets ricocheting from side to side. That would only ratchet up her anxiety. In any case, Brittany had kept her cool. So far.

As Claws crept back into view, he turned and Eve could study his side and back. He had the AR-15 in his arms. A pistol secured in a holster on his belt. A knife strapped to his thigh. A camo backpack with twin water bottles stuffed into net pouches. His balaclava cinched under his belt. He paused again, lifted a baseball cap from his forehead, and brushed the sweat away with his wrist.

She wondered about his dexterity. She could see the fingers of his right hand had been cut as if a power saw had severed them all in one, quick chop. All that remained of his pinky was a tiny stub. The cut had sheared off his ring and middle fingers in a rising slope that ended at his trigger finger. Despite the missing nail on his index finger, she knew he could still exert enough leverage to fire his weapon as well as anyone with proper training and experience. And Claws looked like he possessed plenty of both.

Finally, he spoke. "Brittany Swank, I know you're in there." He pulled the hat down over his forehead and drew a small slip of clear plastic from his shirt pocket. "You left me a trail a mile wide. You know that? This here wrapper I found lying by the big rock upriver. It says *Courtesy of Big River Resort.* I never guessed someone like you'd be a litter bugger like that."

He paused as if he had to decide how to continue.

"Ha-ha-ha!" He let out a static, mechanical laugh, then cut it short. "Plus, you left footprints heading straight up the bank here right into the cabin. You get it?" He wiped his wrist over his mouth. "Okay, so this only goes two ways then. Easy or hard."

Eve winced at the cliché. He paused again and she now saw a vulnerable spot. His kidneys. His backpack didn't cover the space below his ribs and his vest didn't ride low enough to protect him. Her fingers flexed around the steel beam. He stood about ten paces away. If Brittany distracted him, Eve could be on him in seconds.

"The easy way is you come out soft and sweet. Jus' like a ladybug." Another inert chortle. "Hard way's me coming in there for you. And that will piss me off. Piss me off wetly. Which you don't wanna see."

A moment passed in silence.

"Okay, darlin'. I'm gonna count out from ten. You best be out here before I hit five."

A breath. "Ten. Nine. Eight, sev — "

"Okay, stop. Stop! I can't take any more," Brittany pleaded. Her words sounded distant, disembodied. "Something's wrong with my medicine," she begged in a low whimpering cry. "I can't think straight."

"What kind of medicine?" Claws paused to think. "You got Covid?"

"Insulin. I'm diabetic."

This seemed to relieve some anxiety. "All right. Just lie on the floor in there. You got that?"

Eve could hear her shuffling along the floor toward the door.

"I said, you got that?"

"Yeah. I'm on the floor."

"All right then. And you jus' stay that way."

Claws aimed his rifle at the side wall. As he approached the porch he angled the barrel toward the door. Three paces from the deck, a trap sprung and tore into the sides of his right foot.

"Fuck!"

As he scrambled to free his boot from the trap, he twisted to the left and fell onto his side. He braced himself against his rifle, then as he tried to gain some leverage, the AR-15 fired a spray of bullets through the charred remains of the roof.

Eve leaped forward. But before she could reach Claws, she saw Brittany flying through the door with a bed rail clasped in both hands like a spear. She ran two, three, four paces, then tripped as a plank gave way underfoot. She used the rail to pull herself free, then jumped to the ground and drove her weapon into Claws' ribs.

"Fuuuuck!" he wheezed. The blow knocked the wind from him.

Now Eve was on him and slashed her weapon across the side of his neck. As he fell he turned toward her. His eyes seemed to swim in their sockets. Had he fallen into a seizure? Eve didn't waste any time. She kicked the butt of the AR-15 toward Brittany.

"Pick it up and point it at his face."

"But I" — she panted as if she'd run out of breath — "I never even — "

"Doesn't matter," Eve cut her off. "Keep your finger beside the trigger and point it at him. And look like you wanna kill him."

Eve leaned over his head. She could see his chest heaving. Sure enough, Brittany's blow had knocked the air from his lungs. She knew she had less than a minute before he'd recover. Unless a seizure had taken hold of his brain — in which case, he might be gone for good. She unclipped his pistol from its holster and slipped it into the back of her belt. Then she uncinched the knife and sheath from his thigh.

He let out another puff of air and turned onto his left side. Now she could see the beartrap that had snared his boot. As he fell, the leaves and branches covering the spiked jaws had flown into the air. A long chain anchored the steel vice to a post under the porch. Had the jagged teeth penetrated the leather boot and cut into his flesh? If it did, she knew that without medication he'd soon be suffering from infection.

His low moans suggested he was recovering. His eyes wavered as he tried to focus on Eve.

Before he could climb to his feet, she tugged the backpack from his shoulders and tossed it behind her. She took a moment to study his face. One ugly dawg. The skin above his beard flecked with blackheads. His nose punched to one side in some brawl. His ears smeared with dirt. His combat jacket had been torn open at the chest and revealed a crippled Icom two-way radio transceiver. It looked like an eighteen-wheeler had crushed it on the I-5.

"Looks like someone already took a whack at you today."

"Up yours," he wheezed.

She smiled and turned to Brittany.

"Keep the rifle on his face." Her voice was even, controlled. She wanted to assure Brittany that they held command of the situation. "Put two fingers on the trigger guard. That's all he needs to see."

She opened the backpack and rummaged through the contents. Another magazine clip for the pistol, a first aid kit, and four plastic zip ties. In a side pouch, she found two meals of FSRs — first-strike rations — designed to provide basic calories during combat.

She strapped a zip tie around Claw's wrists and slipped the others back into the pack. Her's now. Then she strapped the pack over her shoulders and tucked the knife in the back of her belt. She examined the pistol. A SIG Sauer P226. During her years in the SFPD, the Sig26 had been her assigned sidearm. She'd never fired it on duty, but she knew the weapon inside out. She stood next to Claws's foot, a yard or two from where the trap chain led to the porch post. When his eyes drifted up to face her, she released the magazine, inspected it, and reinserted it into the pistol. The lingering scent of gunshot residue suggested it had been fired in the last day or two. If he'd fired the pistol earlier, he'd reloaded it before he reached the cabin. It was locked and loaded.

"You know when I was a beat cop on the SFPD, the Sig26 was my sidearm." She waited for Claws to absorb the message. "Practiced every week with it. I got so good, I could take out the inner ring on the bull's eye nine times outta ten."

"Yeah-yeah," he muttered and tried to shake the trap from his boot.

"Uhh-uhh. None of that." She pointed the gun at his toes, then tilted her hand toward the river and fired a single round. The shot careened off a rock and smacked into a tree. *Whack.*

"Got your attention?"

He shuddered and sneered with a look of disbelief. Disarmed by two chicks in the middle of nowhere. He studied the zip tie around his wrists and blew out a gust of air. Could this be happening? "Don't matter what you got. In the end, you're fucked. The two of yous."

"Better to worry about yourself. But you do have a way out of this, Claws."

He coughed up a bleak chuckle.

"Tell me where the Hummer is, then Brit and I will be on our way."

"The Hummer?"

"Yeah. Where'd you park it?"

He sucked in a gulp of air and ground his teeth together. "Get this thing offa me!"

"Starting to pinch, is it?" She taunted him with a smile. Then her expression became serious. "Where's the Hummer?"

"The Hummer?" He scoffed and swung his hands to his chest. "Get me outta the zip tie and I might tell you."

Eve narrowed her eyes and took a step to one side. She leveled the Sig26 at his foot and aligned the pistol sight with her right eye.

"How 'bout I take off your little toe first. Make it match the nubs on your hand. Would that suit you?"

Claws shuffled his foot to one side, but the clamp held it in place.

"Hey. That's not smart. You move around like that and I could end up taking your whole foot off."

"Fuck you!"

Eve adjusted her stance, drew a bead on his left foot, lowered the pistol one or two degrees, and fired a round into the heel of his boot. It disintegrated as the bullet ripped the heel away from the shank.

"Hey!" Claws looked as if he could jump out of his skin. "All right! Enough of this shit!"

"Where's the Hummer?"

He blinked, then shifted his gaze to the ground. He expelled a heavy sigh of disgust and turned his attention to Eve. "Parked in the maintenance lot."

Eve studied his face. The pain from the steel teeth biting into his foot was beginning to tell. Of course. The maintenance yard stood at the end of a dirt road about a mile from the resort entrance. "What about the keys?"

"No! First, you cut the zip tie!" he screamed.

Eve shook her head and fired another round into the dirt beside his knee.

"Okay. *Okay.* Under the sun visor. Driver side," he moaned. Then as if he couldn't tolerate his betrayal, he screamed again. *"Fuck!"*

Eve took two steps away and leveled her weapon at his head. "Back at the resort Skipper said the revolution has started. Remember that?" She paused. "Well in this war, asshole, we take no prisoners."

Claws stared into his hands, his spirit broken.

She glanced over her shoulder. "Brit, grab anything you need from the shack. We're heading out."

Brittany slipped the handguard of the AR-15 into the crook of her left arm. After a moment she found the balance point and nodded to Eve. "Got it." She stepped onto the porch and picked her way along the rotting planks to the door. A moment later she returned with her pack strapped to her back.

"Ready," she said.

"Okay."

Eve tugged one of the two water bottles from Claws' pack. She set it on the ground beside his injured foot.

"There's enough water to last until the FBI picks you up. *Maybe.*" She adjusted her backpack and leaned forward. "But listen up. If you come at us again, I will kill you. Either me or my husband. You got that?"

He snarled and tried to free his foot again.

"You got that, Claws?" Her eyes narrowed. "*I will kill you.*"

CHAPTER THIRTEEN

WHEN THE DOOR closed behind Eve, Finch reached into the pile of hostages' shoes and slipped his runners onto his feet. Then he jogged to the doorway that led into the lodge corridor. He pushed through the crowd who were bottled up by Dogboy. Finch tugged a fire extinguisher from the wall bracket and snapped the nozzle free from the stay.

Dogboy stood his ground with his AR-15 braced in his arms. Finch could see the safety was engaged, but nonetheless, Dogboy's voice sent tremors through the crowd.

"Everyone down!" he screamed as he pointed the rifle muzzle to the floor. "Or the next rounds go into your feet!"

Finch shook his head and pressed forward. "Lemme through," he said, his voice steely with determination. "Unless we gut the fire in the next five minutes the whole building'll go up!"

Dogboy's mouth gaped open as he tried to assess the situation. A look of utter confusion washed over his face. Wasn't Finch the last man out of the can? "Yeah, okay," he conceded.

"Go for it."

As Finch elbowed his way into the corridor, two bursts from Skipper's AR-15 ripped into the ceiling. "Everybody, back to where you were!"

His command drew a new round of whimpers and cries as the hostages filed back to where they'd hunched on the floor and leaned against the circular wall of the Rotunda.

As the siren wailed, smoke streamed through the cracks between the men's room door and the doorframe. Finch knew the door would be too hot to touch. He also knew that he had to kill the fire before the flames breached the bathroom into the hallway. He pulled the release pin on the extinguisher and set it on the floor. To his left stood a decorative coat tree, the top pegs carved to resemble deer antlers. He held it by the base and pressed the antlers against the swing door. It budged an inch and a cloud of black smoke surged into the corridor.

"Dogboy, get over here and push the door open!"

Skipper stepped into the corridor next to Dogboy. When he witnessed Finch taking control, he yelled into Dogboy's ear. "Give him a hand! *Go!*" His voice vibrated with a sense of impending catastrophe. He seized Dogboy's rifle in his right hand and shoved him toward the bathroom door.

Dogboy grabbed the coat tree from Finch and nodded to him.

"Okay," Finch said. "When you open the door expect a gust of flames to come at us. First, the fire will billow, then fade back. When it fades, I'll go in." He grasped the tank of the extinguisher in his right hand, the hose in his left. "Got it?"

Dogboy nodded. "Okay, now." He pressed the door open.

Another cloud of smoke swept up to the ceiling followed by a wide tongue of flames licking at the walls.

"All the way!" Finch commanded.

Dogboy charged forward. A tower of flames exploded toward them. Dogboy held his position. Before the flames could take another breath Finch pulled the release lever on the hose. A white jet of sodium bicarbonate surged from the nozzle. Finch took a moment to gain control of the hose, drew a breath, then pushed past Dogboy into the bathroom. He sprayed the path ahead of him as he made his way to the stall where he'd set the fire. Impressed by its effectiveness, he hosed down the entire enclosure until the flames were smothered. He continued to spray the walls and ceiling until a last spurt dribbled from the extinguisher's nozzle. While he'd fought the blaze and brought it under control, he managed to hold his breath for a minute or two, but now the intoxicating wood smoke began to choke him. He tugged a handkerchief from his back pocket, soaked it in the toilet bowl, and held it over his nose and mouth.

As he dipped over the toilet he realized the fire had opened a seam in the back of the stall. The gap allowed the fire to breathe again and it bounced back to life. Finch caught a glimpse of the far side of the partition. The kitchen.

"Dogboy, there's a breach. Get into the kitchen. Douse the fuckin' thing from the other side of the wall!"

As he waited for Dogboy to dampen the flames in the kitchen, his coughing finally abated and he heard the ongoing screams of two or three other sirens emanating from the lobby, kitchen, and Rotunda. Below their high-pitched wailing, he

could make out the cries from the hostages who'd been corralled into the Rotunda. Were they safe? God help you if
they're not, he told himself. You'll have the lives of thirty souls
on your hands.

When a spray of foam blew through the gap into the toilet
stall, he knew Dogboy had snuffed the flames in the kitchen.
"Thank God," he muttered. The kitchen would be loaded with
flammable oils and propane or natural gas burners. A bomb
fused to destroy the entire building. If a fireball exploded there,
the surrounding forest would ignite a wildfire that would rip
through the valley all the way up to Snow Mountain and down
to Mendocino.

His eyes weeping from smoke and the bitter fumes of the
sodium bicarbonate, he dropped the extinguisher and clasped
the handkerchief tight to his face. Eyes closed, he ran his free
hand over the stall door and followed the wall out into the
hallway. He stumbled over the hat tree that Dogboy had tossed
aside, recovered his footing, and felt his way down the corridor
to the lobby. His eyes blinked open. The stinging smoke made
him wince. Across the foyer, he could make out the wide glass
doors leading outside and made his way onto the porch where
he bumped against a deck chair. He sat on the lip of the verandah, drew a breath, and coughed as his legs spread in a V along
the wood planks. He coughed and coughed again. A moment of
panic seized him when he couldn't get enough air. As he struggled to control his breathing, he wiped the handkerchief over
his eyes.

Then he glimpsed an opportunity. Twenty yards past the
parking lot stood a few manzanita trees that lined the front of

the forest. If he could make his way into the bush, perhaps he could find Eve. She'd escaped less than half an hour ago. Together they could make their way back to Mendocino and call in the FBI. How long would it take them to mobilize a SWAT team? Maybe three or four hours.

He pulled himself to his feet. When he recovered his balance he walked across the gravel lot toward a Ford Bronco. Maybe best to steal a vehicle. No, find Eve first. He started to jog toward the forest when he heard a burst of gunfire behind him. Five or six rocks jumped to life at his feet, then drifted back to earth in puffs of smoke that had pulverized them.

"Finch! Next five rounds go into your spine!"

He blinked. No mistaking Skipper's voice. Or his deadly intentions. He lifted his hands in the air and swung around to face his tormentor.

"You got me, Skipper." He tried to put on a smile but began another round of coughing.

"Yeah. I do." He frowned with a thin-lip expression that revealed a mix of hatred and raw anger. "Come here, asshole."

Finch shook his head and made his way back to the lodge verandah. Every step ushered more wheezing from his chest. He glanced at Skipper, hoping to see a trace of sympathy on his face.

"Now pull off those shoes and get back into the Rotunda while I figure out what the fuck happened in there."

Finch sat on the porch step. As he slipped off his shoes, Skipper stood above him threatening to smash his head with the butt of his weapon.

"You know Finch, you really think you're something special, don't you? But the truth is you're just another worm digging his way through the dirt."

Finch glanced at Skipper's face and decided not to respond. Not yet. His time would come. Better to gather his shoes and limp back to the Rotunda and try to sleep.

Chapter Fourteen

Weary from the firefight and lack of sleep, Finch slouched against one of the floor-level windows in the Rotunda. His fingers traced the steri-strips that covered the cut on his forehead. At least the headache is fading, he thought, as he watched Jasper marshal the resort staff from the kitchen back into the circular room. Roland Clapp trudged along the floor with a carafe of coffee weighing each hand down. His wife held two stacks of paper cups in her hands. The other staffers — Michaels, the head of maintenance, Finnegan the chef, and Randy Salter the night auditor — carried trays loaded with sandwiches. None of them appeared affected by the smoke. Finch assumed that Dogboy had snuffed the flames before the fire caused any substantial damage.

After he'd ordered Finch back into the lodge, Skipper marched into the kitchen to assess the damage. Once again he'd divided his team.

Finch dabbed his eyes with his handkerchief. Fortunately, his eyesight had cleared and he took a moment to study the two terrorists before him. Dogboy and Jasper still wore balaclavas. Despite everything, they maintained good discipline, he thought.

Jasper directed the staff to load the food and coffee onto a table at the far end of the stage. After they returned to the floor, Dogboy walked to the center of the circle. His rifle hung from his shoulder by the gun strap. He held a clipboard and pen in his hands.

"Okay. Listen up. Everyone gets one sandwich and one cuppa coffee. Come up one at a time when I call your name." His eyes scanned the hostages, then he studied the names on the clipboard. "First up, Nancy Greenlaw."

A murmur bubbled through the crowd.

"Nancy Greenlaw!"

Next to the door where Eve had made her escape, Nancy pulled herself to her feet and took a step toward Dogboy. "Here." She waved a hand in the air.

Dogboy checked off her name as Nancy took a sandwich, then pumped a cup of coffee from the steel thermos.

"Next, Jenny Wexler."

Jenny exchanged an apprehensive look with her husband, walked to the stage, and took her sandwich and coffee.

Dogboy checked her name.

"Vic Wexler."

Another check, another sandwich, another cup of coffee. As the hostages filed back and forth with their rations, Finch considered their captors. Claws, presumably still tracking Brittany Swank in the bush, appeared to be missing in action. The odds had improved somewhat. Three against thirty. Maybe he could enhance his chances of escape with a new gambit.

But that thought vanished the instant he heard Dogboy call Eve's name.

"Eve Noon," he repeated as he scanned the room. He blinked, then turned to Finch.

"Where is she?"

"I don't know." He shrugged. "You and I were putting out the fire…" His voice trailed off. "I haven't seen her since."

"What?"

"Honest. I don't know." He shook his head with a mystified expression. "Maybe check our cabin? The Sugar Pine," he added as if he wanted to find her every bit as much as Dogboy.

Dogboy let out an exasperated sigh. "Jasper. Go tell Skipper Eve Noon is missing." He crooked his thumb in the direction of the kitchen. "Then check if she's in Sugar Pine Cottage."

"What?" Her voice had a defiant edge. As if she wondered if their mission had run off track.

"You heard me."

"Screw this," she muttered, wheeled around, and made her way to the kitchen.

CHAPTER FIFTEEN

JASPER FOUND SKIPPER alone in the kitchen sorting through the debris from the fire. He'd pulled a rack of dishes away from the scorched wall and was on his knees probing the singed wood and drywall with a pair of heavy-duty tongs. When he heard her approach he stood up, yanked off his balaclava, and rubbed a hand over his face. The narrow scar that sank below his jawline from his right ear — a wound embedded in his weathered face — appeared raw and sore.

"No way the fire started on this side of the wall." He pointed to the wall with the tongs.

She leaned forward to examine the damage and the piles of foamy fire retardant splashed on the floor. "You sure?"

"No way," he insisted. A new thought came to mind. "And what the hell are you doing here? I ordered you and Dogboy to mind the scum."

The scum. Jasper was tired of hearing the word. She pointed to the Rotunda room. "Eve Noon's missing."

"What the fuck?" In a fit, he threw the steel tongs across

the room. They crashed against a row of frying pans hanging above the stove and rattled onto a prep table and the floor. "Since when?"

"The fire, I guess." She shook her head. "Look, Skipper, does it really matter?"

"What'd'ya mean?" He peered down at her. "Of course it fucking matters."

She started to pace across the room, then turned back to confront him. "It's about the strategy. *We're just supposed to scare the shit out of them.* That's the goal. That's what you told us." She paused. "We've done that, right? Half of them are in tears. Maybe it's time to call Claws in and push out of here before Eve Noon or Brittany Swank reach the cops."

"Pull yourself together Jasper." He held up two fingers. "Two things. One. *Half* of them in tears? Fuck that noise, we're not done here until all of them have completely shit their pants." He glared at her to ensure she absorbed his message.

"Two. Claws is out of range. I tried to call him on the Icom. He didn't pick up."

"What about now?" Her voice freighted with concern.

"Like I said." He shook his head. The hint of her insubordination needled him. "I tried ten minutes ago. Nothing."

"Nothing?"

"Look, I know about you and Claws."

Her eyes narrowed as she studied his face. "What does that mean?"

"Listen up. How many times have we gone over this? Ten? Fifteen? You know not to let personal crap interfere with the mission."

The mission? The words almost made her choke. There'd be no mission without the forces to execute it. She rolled her lips together as she tried to cool her temper. Best not to say anything. Try a different approach. "Dogboy says I should go down to the Sugar Pine cottage. See if Noon's down there."

Skipper's eyes shifted to the right, then back. "Yeah, maybe. But make it quick. I'll go back to the Rotunda and mind the scum with Dogboy." He examined her as if he needed to confirm her commitment. "You good with that?"

"Yeah, I'm good." She made a mock, two-finger salute, turned toward the reception hall, and walked out the front door onto the gravel path that led down to the row of cottages. She clutched her baton in her right hand and tapped it against her thigh as she walked. The soft tap-tap-tap helped her think. Exactly when did the plan start unraveling? Since Claws had been dispatched to find Brittany Swank. The moment he left they were short-handed. What was Skipper thinking to send Claws after the chick-girl and leave them one man down? None of them — Claws, Dogboy, or Jasper herself — were included in the strategy meeting with the First Freedom Corps. Nope, it had all filtered down from the Corps through Skipper alone. "Our orders are to scare the shit out of the media scum for two days. *And two nights,*" he'd told them. "Let the scum know the revolution has started. But nobody gets hurt. Just like they say. No harm, no foul. Then we roll out of there when everyone's asleep. Monday morning, oh-two hundred hours. Disappear like a puff of smoke."

"A fuckin' puff of smoke," she mumbled as she reached the Sugar Pine cottage. "Instead we just about burn the whole place down."

She knew the kitchen fire was Skipper's fault. Or at least his reaction to it. With a man down, some firebug took his best shot and hit the mark. Who was it?

The Sugar Pine door, unlocked, swung open when she nudged it with the baton. She did a quick sweep of the bathroom, kitchenette, and living room. All empty. The acorn stove contained a spool of gray ash — the remains of a fire log. Romantic. But no sign of Eve Noon here, she whispered to herself. She walked to the bedroom and leaned against the door frame. The sheets and duvet were tossed aside. A pillow on the floor. She inhaled the musty scent in the air. Sex. Yeah, of course. She enjoyed the same thing two nights ago with Claws. A rough-and-tumble roll behind the woodshed. The way they both liked it. She smiled. He was the ugliest man she'd ever met. Which meant she never had to worry about wandering eyes. Few other women would have him. And he knew that she had eyes for him forever.

She opened the mini-fridge and ran her hand over the row of beer cans. Not her thing. She opened the bottle of OJ, grabbed a pack of nuts, and sat on the sofa. What to do? She slipped a handful of nuts into her mouth, ground them between her teeth, and washed them down with the juice. As she gazed through the sliding glass doors past the patio and into the forest she understood the appeal of the place. A bit of paradise, here. If only Skipper hadn't screwed it up so bad.

She finished eating the pack of nuts and drank half the bottle of juice. So, what next? Head back to the lodge and talk to Dogboy. Maybe he could see the situation for what it was now. Their job was done, time to move out. The two of them should let Skipper know the game was over. Mission accomplished. Everyone was totally scared shitless. Including her.

CHAPTER SIXTEEN

"FINCH!"

The sound of his name piercing the air shook Will out of his reverie. The throbbing in his head had returned and driven him to find relief in remembrances of better times. As he sat perched against the wall of the Rotunda, he felt his past life sinking into the pool of lost memories. Lying on Waikiki Beach with Eve at his side. Cuddling their baby Casey as she slept through a winter windstorm back in their cottage on Telegraph Hill. Had all that really happened or was it just a series of illusions?

He ran two fingers over the steri-strips that Eve had taped over the cut on his forehead and gazed at the clock above the dome entrance. It showed the day and time. Saturday, 6:37 AM. Just a few hours since Eve's escape.

Skipper stood in the entryway and pointed a calloused finger at him. "Finch! Get over here!"

"What?" He could barely hear his own voice. He felt tired, hungry, sore. His lungs still wheezed from smoke inhalation.

Skipper pumped his baton in his open palm and took three steps toward Finch. Far enough to alert Finch that he needed to come to full attention. He struggled to stand up and move away from his tormentor. The varnished wood floor felt cold on his bare feet.

"Come with me." Skipper grabbed Finch's shirt collar and tugged him toward the lobby. They skirted behind the reception desk, down a short hallway, and into the kitchen. Skipper prodded him with the truncheon until they reached the scorched breach in the wall that opened into the bathroom where Finch had ignited the fire.

"Sit." He pushed him to the floor and nudged Finch's chin with the baton so that his face looked into the charred hole in the wall.

"Fire didn't start here," he announced.

"No?"

A look of angry disbelief filled Skipper's eyes. Under the balaclava, Finch could detect his growing rage. "No. I spent the last ten minutes running this down." His larynx bobbled as he spoke. "You know, I'm a specialist in arson forensics."

"Is that right?" His eyes swept over Skipper's mask. He knew he had to keep him talking.

"It is. And I know for a fact that this fire was set in the can." His thumb hooked toward the far side of the wall. "Have a look and you'll see what I mean."

Another prod from the club pressed Finch's nose into the gap in the wall. He could see the remains of the toilet paper dispenser where he'd ignited his firebomb. Smell the charred wood and plasterboard. He choked down another gulp of smokey air. Poison.

"I see what you mean," he said, drawing his head back from the wall and looking up at Skipper's masked face. "So what happened?"

"Give me a fucking break, Finch. You were the last person in there. You set the fire so Eve could slip away. I'm not stupid."

Finch believed him. Not stupid at all. He was beginning to believe the interrogation might end badly.

"Just so you know, Claws took her down an hour ago. Your wife and that girly-girl, Swank."

Finch blinked. All his hopes were pinned on Eve. On her escape. On the chance that she could call in the FBI. He glanced at the row of knives clamped to a magnetic bar next to the stove. Six steps away, an eight-inch carving knife. But first, he had to stand up. Maybe point to another explanation for the fire to Skipper. Something to allow him to climb to his feet.

"Look, Skipper — "

"Shut the fuck up." With the butt of his truncheon, he tapped the steri-strips on Finch's forehead. "Not another word."

Finch felt a chill run through his arms as he watched Skipper pull his Icom from a pocket and speak to someone. Moments later he heard the kitchen door swing open. Jasper approached them. When she saw Finch squatting on the floor below Skipper, her eyes narrowed with a puzzled look.

"What'd you need, Skip?"

"Got the duct tape?"

She nodded.

"And zip ties?"

She shrugged. "Only the one." She pulled a single twenty-inch black zip tie from a pocket.

Skipper shook his head with a hint of dismay. "Okay, that'll have to do."

As he heard them speak, the chill running through Finch turned into a deep shudder.

"Check your Glock."

"What?"

"Draw your gun and put a round in the chamber."

Finch watched as Jasper's lips curled into a frown. Her eyes revealed a look of dismay. She hesitated, then drew her pistol from the belt holster and showed it to Skipper. She seemed confused. Did he simply want to inspect her weapon? Or was he playing some kind of mind game?

"Chamber a round," he said, his voice barely a whisper. "Then tap the back of his head."

Finch heard the bullet click into the chamber.

"Skip, I'm not sure — "

"I said, tap the back of his fuckin' head!"

She took a step toward the wall and leveled the Glock at Finch.

"You mean…"

Again, Skipper's mood turned raw, in addition to Finch's ploy, now he had to tolerate insubordination bordering on treason. "Just hold the muzzle to his skull. You get that?"

Finch heard her draw a long breath. Then he felt the machined muzzle of the weapon press against his head. A perfect, nine-millimeter-wide circle of steel.

"Now listen up, Finch." His voice cold again. "You make a

move and Jasper's going to unload her Glock into your head." A faint smile appeared through the Balaclava. "You got that?"

Finch managed to nod. Then he muttered a weak gasp. "Yeah."

"Pass me the tape."

Jasper handed the duct tape to her boss. He peeled off a foot-long strip, bit into the edge with his teeth, and ripped it from the spool. Then he leaned over, wrapped the tape across Finch's mouth, and secured it under his ears. He took a moment to examine his handiwork, then glanced at Jasper.

"Gi'me the tie."

He stretched it end-to-end to assure himself that it was long enough to do the job. "Finch. Hands in front."

Finch's arms quaked as he tried to gain control of his situation. He realized he might get one more chance. If he was bound and gagged, they wouldn't kill him here. Not in the kitchen. Maybe they'd lead him back to the Rotunda where they could make an example of him. Or lead him into the forest, then dispatch him. He tried to decide which was better. A private or public execution? The absurd debate ended when Skipper drove the butt of his truncheon into Finch's chest.

"Finch! Hands out front!"

He doubled over, snorted, and then managed to right himself. As he presented his hands, a final thought came to mind. The time he'd watched two cops from the SFPD zip tie a man's hands following a carjacking. The carjacker clenched his fists and butted his hands together at the widest possible disposition. Thumb-to-thumb. The cops loaded him into the back of their squad car. When they reached their station and opened the back door, they were surprised when the perp leaped from the car — hands-free — and made a run for the street. Fortunately, the gate was locked and they took him down in a tag-team quarterback sack. But the guy had freed his hands and made a run for it. So maybe…

Skipper pulled the zip tight around Finch's wrists.

"All right. Take him out back" — his left arm swung toward the emergency exit that led toward the food storage shed and the A-frame — "then put him down."

Again Jasper paused. "You mean — "

"I mean," Skipper interrupted her as if he couldn't tolerate another word of defiance, "you take him out to the back. And I want every scum in the hall to hear the sound of a bullet smashing through his head. No. Make that *two* rounds. *Do you get that?"*

This time she didn't hesitate. "Okay, Skipper. Got it."

"For once." He drew a hand down the length of his mask as if he had to consider his next steps.

CHAPTER SEVENTEEN

JASPER GUIDED FINCH past the propane tank which fueled the kitchen stoves, through the emergency exit, and onto a gravel path that led to the A-frame cabin. As they walked, the stones underfoot cut into the soles of his feet. He winced but turned his attention to his hands. Turn them, he said to himself. Turn them so that the palms face each other. He felt a bit of slack as the zip tie loosened. Slightly. But to free himself, he knew he'd have to grind his wrists against the plastic strap.

He stumbled past an outdoor food storage locker. A fan whirled lazily on the top of the concrete structure. The door was ajar, an open padlock dangled from the hasp. As they approached the A-frame, he considered running for the front door, but the pain in his feet kept him plodding forward.

"Over there," Jasper pointed her gun past the back of the A-frame. Twenty or thirty feet beyond the cabin, the forest rose above them into the empty sky. Finch could barely think as he walked toward his place of execution. Skipper had ordered her to take him into the woods and "put him down." To kill him?

Neither Skipper nor Jasper seemed able to say the words aloud.

Two stairs climbed from the path up to a narrow porch that led to a sliding glass door at the rear of the A-frame. A sheer curtain wafted in and out of a gap between the door and the frame. Finch wondered if the maintenance manager, Michaels, might be inside. Or perhaps Eve was there, waiting for the cops to arrive. He knew Skipper had lied about Claws taking her down. Claws was nowhere to be seen. His disappearance offered some hope.

"Keep going," Jasper whispered as she poked her pistol into his spine. "Into the woods."

Finch wrestled with the zip tie binding his wrists. He could feel the band loosen as his flesh began to tear against the plastic. Maybe it would work. If he could free his hands, then when Jasper made a move he could swing around and wrestle the gun from her.

"'nother twenty yards, Finch. See those birch trees? Head over there."

Finch wrenched his wrists together. A drizzle of blood seeped down his fingers. Damn it. How had the carjacker done it? He didn't have time to work his hands free. Okay, same game plan, he told himself. There'll come a time. Maybe only a second. One second when you swing around and double-fist her in the head. As he approached the birch trees, he wove his fingers together to form a club.

"Here," Jasper announced. She scraped some dried birch leaves aside with her boot. "This is far enough. In fact, this whole fuckin' thing has gone far enough."

"What?" he mumbled through the duct tape. His lips may

as well have been glued together. He turned to her and shrugged to show her he had no idea what she wanted.

"Down on your knees."

Now, he told himself. *Now!* Finch swung around, his fists reaching for her head. She arched backward and stepped away from the blow. Finch's momentum threw him off balance. He fell to his knees and onto his belly.

"What the fuck was that?!" She choked back a laugh.

Finch crawled toward the nearest tree, a young birch. The trunk was thin, maybe six inches in diameter.

"Guess I would've tried that too. When it comes down to it, we're all worms. Or just waitin' for the day they take over." Her voice held a note of sympathy.

"Stay down on your belly, Finch. This is where this fuckin' clusterfuck comes to an end."

Unable to comprehend what she meant, he gasped through his nose to try to clear the dust from his nostrils. He knew his feet were bleeding. Everything had gone wrong. Was this the end? Here, crawling over twigs and dry leaves.

"All right, feet together."

Something was changing. Her voice revealed something new, a secret he couldn't decode.

"Look, I'm not going to fucking shoot you. But Skipper has to believe I did. That's why we're out here in the sticks." She kicked the soles of his feet. "Now ankles together. For both our sakes, I gotta strap you up."

She pulled another zip tie from her pocket. She'd lied to Skipper about that. He could see it now. She was rebelling against Skipper. Rebelling against the revolution.

"First nudge your head up to the trunk of the tree," she added. "Then give me your foot."

He realized that his only way out was to trust her. Maybe she had a plan, too. He decided to follow her lead and crawled a few inches forward until his forehead touched the base of the tree. Then he drew his legs together. He felt her grasp his pant cuffs, then loop the zip tie around them. He heard the zip tie click as she snugged it tight. Then he tried to pull his legs up toward his waist.

"Don't do that. Just do as I say," she warned him. "Now put your hands out to your side. Be good and I'll cut you free."

He looked over his shoulder and saw her draw a multitool from a pouch on her belt. He watched as she unfolded a blade from the handle. He rolled to one side and brought his hands out from under his stomach. She leaned forward and cut the tie, then immediately swung around to the other side of the tree and tugged both of his arms forward so that they encircled the trunk. As she prepared to fasten a new zip tie around his hands, he held his wrists out, again thumb-to-thumb, just as the carjacker had done. Jasper struggled to cinch the tie together. After a moment he heard the plastic lock click.

He was now lying on his belly, his hands encircling the young birch tree. A new panic seized him and he struggled to control his breathing and assess his situation. His head nodded against the base of the tree. His hands and feet were bound, his mouth gagged. Finally, a single clear thought entered his mind: Settle down and you might live.

"Now look, Finch. This whole shit show's gonna be over after tomorrow. But before we leave I'm gonna unstrap you.

Middle of the night on Monday morning. You understand?"

Finch blinked once.

"You think you can last that long?"

He blinked again.

"Good. Your only chance of stayin' alive is if Skipper thinks you're dead. *You get that?* Dead. And if you get loose somehow or 'nother, don't peel that tape off your mouth. If he hears one peep from you Skipper'll come and kill you himself. An' me next," she added as if this warning sealed her alliance with him.

Finch then heard her stand and her boots crush the dirt and desiccated leaves as she moved three or four paces toward the A-frame. Seconds later he heard her fire a round from her Glock into the open air. The sound rang across the yard to the Rotunda and echoed back into the forest. Then she fired a second bullet into the air. Again the echo reverberated through the resort. Thank God for that, he thought. The pistol reports meant he was still alive.

Chapter Eighteen

CLAWS SPAT ONTO the ground and watched the women descend the slope to the deer trail along the river bank. They turned right, upstream, back toward the big rock. He could hear their shoes clatter against the stones, then a distant chirp of laughter from them. He waited for the sound of their chatter to fade then drew his left knee toward his chest. He looped his cuffed hands over his knee and began to unlace the boot. It took him over twenty minutes to slip it off and uncover the knife he kept tucked into the backstay. He pinched the pocket knife — a Swiss Army miniature — between his thumb and the tip of his forefinger and opened the two-inch blade. It wasn't easy, sawing the knife back and forth between his wrists against the zip tie. Twice the tiny knife slipped from his fingers into his lap. Careful, he whispered to himself. Drop it in the dirt and it'll be outta reach.

But by the time dusk fell, he'd cut the plastic band in half. He leaned forward to pry open the trap that ensnared his right foot. "Damn it," he muttered as he examined the shoe. "An honest-to-God bear trap." To free himself he needed to pry apart the twin jaws simultaneously. This was another one of those times when his amputated fingers proved to be a disabling handicap. He struggled to loosen the left jaw but soon realized both sides were hinged together under the midsole of his boot. He had to open one at the same time as the other, or neither one would budge. As he played with the jaws of the bear trap, slivers of pain darted up his legs.

He swept his arms behind his back, planted his hands in the dirt, and studied the problem. When nothing came to mind he gave the trap a good kick with his left foot. The chain danced in the air. Right. The chain was anchored to a post under the porch. No need to sit here. He pulled himself onto his knees and wobbled as he tried to stand. It didn't help that Eve fuckin' Noon had shot off the heel on his other boot. He steadied himself with one of the bed rails the women had tossed away, then used it to hop over to the porch where he sat on the first step. When it groaned under his weight he shifted his butt next to the cabin siding where he guessed the joist might be more sturdy.

He leaned against the exterior wall and gulped down a slug of water while he considered his options. He gazed at the snare and the chain which ran out of sight below the porch. Then the solution dawned on him.

"What an idiot!" he moaned. In seconds, he unlaced his boot, pulled his foot free, and propped it on his left knee. He massaged his heel, his ankles. Next, he peeled off his sock.

"Jesus," he muttered as he examined his punctured skin. The teeth had penetrated the leather boot and left a straight row of four perforation wounds on each side of his foot just below his ankle. None was bleeding, but he knew that if he didn't treat them, infection could set in. But of course, Eve Noon had stolen his pack and the first aid kit tucked into the back pouch.

Turning to the other foot, he examined the gap where the boot heel was supposed to be. Gone. Torn away by the blast from the P226. "Unbelievable!" he wailed and slapped a hand against the side of his head.

With his right foot injured, and his left boot heel blown away, he knew he'd be hobbling through the forest. And without a flashlight or compass, he'd be traveling blind.

All right. You got two choices, he murmured to himself. Walk out of here tomorrow with one foot wounded, one heel gone. Either that or like Noon said, wait here for the FBI and go straight to prison — *where you will die.* He snarled again, his teeth snapping in the air.

No, better to wait for first light. Get your footing and steer by the sun. Meantime, grab some shuteye, Claws. Tomorrow — Sunday — it'll be do or die. And you're gonna make it do.

He took a moment to free his empty boot from the bear trap, then lifted both by their laces with his good hand, the water bottle with his right, and inched his way along the porch and through the open doorway into the shack. He leaned against the wall next to the stove. He closed his eyes and tried to sleep. Eventually, he slumped onto the floor and pillowed an arm under his head. When the dawn light blinked through the splintered shingles of the roof he knew it was time to move on.

CHAPTER NINETEEN

"SO WHAT CHANGED?"

Eve trudged along the shoreline track and glanced over her shoulder to ensure Brittany kept up. Once they reached the big rock they'd have to cross to the other side of the river and make their way through the forest and back to the resort. Fortunately, Claws kept a compass and flashlight in his pack which Eve had found along with two MREs, some beef jerky, and another water bottle.

"You mean when I came out of the cabin?" Brittany wheezed as she tried to match Eve's pace.

"Uh, no. You didn't just *come out* of the cabin. You clobbered the bastard. It was the last thing I expected."

"Yeah. Me, too." Her fight with Claws astounded her. As she walked along the deer trail she kept reliving the rush, the adrenaline — the mindless attack. What happened? Who was the woman bolting from the shack and spearing the cammie in the ribs? Whoever she'd become did not correspond to the Brittany Swank she knew. Not the persona she so carefully cultivated back in San Fran where she'd become the "queen of the scene" — a domme in the latest hot career niche — a digital influencer. During the pandemic, she'd engineered the media campaigns for a trio of tech start-ups. It took a firm handshake, a hint of lacey cleavage, a flirtatious embrace of tech-bro male dominance, along with a fluent command of digital jargon married to business metaphors like financial algos, top-line cash flow, and second-tranche funding.

But nowhere had she ever caught sight of the insulin-jangled madwoman charging across a rotting porch with a spear in her hands. Then thrusting it into the stomach of a disabled cammie.

"You know what it came down to?"

"What?" Eve adjusted the AR-15 strap on her shoulder. She was used to carrying the weapon now, but it still felt awkward as she walked.

"To Jonny. I couldn't bear the thought of dying out here and leaving him on his own."

"Yeah. I get that. When I made it out of the resort, all I could think about was getting back to my daughter."

"Casey?"

"Uh-huh."

"Same thing."

"Well, whatever it took, Brit, you were a lioness back there."

"A lioness." She laughed at that. "The tech coders call me a cougar. But lioness? Yes, ma'am. Sounds like a promotion to me. I'll take that any day."

"Ha-ha!" Eve couldn't stifle her laughter. In the heady

business world of San Francisco, they both had to shield themselves from what Eve called YMS. Young Male Syndrome. Not long ago she'd turned forty. She could feel the changes in her body. Her fading energy, the slow shedding of something vital. Perhaps her allure was fading, too. But Brit was ten years younger — a cougar, a MILF — all the libidinous nonsense that identified her as fair game to young men yearning for an experienced woman.

"There it is." Brittany pointed up the dry bed creek. In the distance, stood the big rock.

Ten minutes later, they stopped to lean on the massive granite stone and sip some water. Eve tore off a wedge of beef jerky with her teeth and passed the stick to her friend. Brittany gnawed at the tight rope of meat, then tugged off a piece and began to chew it into a pulp. After she swallowed a small wad, she turned to Eve.

"So how'd you escape from the resort?"

"Will. He set up a diversion."

A puzzled look crossed her face. "What kind of diversion?"

Eve related the story of the fire, the hostages' panic, the screaming fire alarms. Followed by her quiet escape through the emergency exit.

"So that's why you have to go back. For Will."

Eve nodded and drank some water. "After what happened with Claws" — she pointed downriver toward the shack — "I knew it would take too long to get to Mendocino on foot. Besides, the cammies are down to three. And now we have weapons. Things are tilting in our favor."

She tipped her chin to the AR-15 strapped to her shoulder.

Eve wore the Sig26 on her hip and still had the knife tucked behind her belt. "And we have access to the Hummer. Once we get that, we'll be in the driver's seat." She smiled. "Literally."

Brittany coughed up a light chuckle to suggest an air of optimism. She knew they were well-armed. Any more weapons would only become a burden. But she could feel a dark passage lay ahead of them. A tunnel with no opening at the far end.

Eve sensed her despair. "Besides, we can get you more insulin, right?"

Brittany nodded and glanced away. During the silence, they both felt her pressing urgency.

"How much time do you have?" Eve asked.

She pursed her lips and blew out a long breath. "I don't know. My cell phone died last night. It has an app that monitors my glucose. Without it, I'm flying blind." She turned her head to gaze at the sky and waved a hand as if she could sweep away all her troubles. "I told you about breaking the backup vial, right?"

"Yeah. You said."

"So without insulin, I might crash," she said with a shrug.

"What are the signs?"

"Forgetting things. Not making sense. Rattling on about nothing. And having to pee all the time."

"But when you get the insulin, how much does it take?"

"Usually 28 units of insulin will bring me back to normal."

"Okay." Eve's face bore a serious look. "And you have more insulin in your cottage. Right?" Stupid question, she thought. Brittany's told you that already. Twice. It was her sole motive for returning to the resort.

"I don't know why I left it." Brittany wiped her eyes with an open hand. Then in an angry tone, she added, "I was so fucking scared, Eve. When I saw them coming for me, I panicked."

"Of course you did. We all did.

Eve set her hand on Brittany's shoulder, and she pulled Eve into a tight embrace.

"Look, we're gonna be okay," Eve whispered into her ear, then stepped away. "But we have to get going. We'll get to the road, then find the Hummer."

Brittany turned to gaze into the forest. "It's getting dark."

"We've got a flashlight." She drew it from her pack and passed it to her friend. "Here, you lead. I'll guide us with the compass. Okay?"

"Yeah." Then she said, "I'm a lioness, right?"

"You are." Eve forced a laugh, then they crossed the riverbed to the north side and Eve took her first reading from the compass.

Despite her determination to press on through the night and Brittany's desperation to reach her insulin supply, after tromping ten or twenty minutes into the black ink of the forest, they both realized it was impossible to advance any further. The risk of spraining an ankle on a tree root, or falling and breaking a limb was obvious.

"Maybe you should use the flashlight and the compass. Like together, I mean," Brittany suggested and handed the lamp to her.

Eve swept the light across the surrounding trees. The forest, thick with waist-high salal, dead roots, and deadfall looked impenetrable. "I don't know, Brit. I can't take a bearing on anything more than five feet away. Even then, there's no way —"

"Yeah, I know," she interrupted and slipped the pack from her shoulders. After walking for two hours, she couldn't bear the weight much longer. "Maybe we should find a place to sit and wait for daylight."

Eve knew it was their only option. "What about the insulin? How're you doing?"

She swallowed a sip of orange juice. "I'm into the juice now" — she waved the bottle and screwed the cap in place — "then ... you know. I've got the raisins for breakfast." She put on a smile that she knew Eve could not see in the dark.

"Okay, let's find a spot."

Eve guided them forward. She was surprised when they stumbled upon a space no more than a hundred feet away. The clearing was surrounded by a stand of birch trees that climbed high into the impenetrable darkness. No moon, no stars. She swept the flashlight a few yards past their feet.

"This good?"

"Yeah." Brittany slipped her pack onto a patch of dry moss.

Eve tugged Claws's backpack from her shoulders, unzipped the large flap, and dug out the thermal blanket she'd noticed back at the shack. She drew it from a plastic sleeve and lay it on the ground. It was bigger than she first imagined. Eight by ten feet, she guessed.

"We can lean together, back to back to preserve our body heat, and wrap this around us."

"You think it'll help?"

"Yeah. Will had to spend a night outside in one of these. He said it worked pretty well."

Brittany shrugged. "Okay. Gotta pee first, though."

"Me, too."

As she relieved herself in the shelter of a fallen tree limb, Brittany wondered about the bears prowling for food. Or mountain lions. Which was worse? Maybe the scent of their urine would mark a boundary of some kind. Did it work like that?

It was one more question she couldn't answer. Like so many solutions that evaded her.

CHAPTER TWENTY

CLAWS EXAMINED HIS right foot and detected the first signs of infection. He pressed his thumb across his skin and smudged away the pus dots surrounding each skin perforation. Then he rolled his socks over his toes and up to his ankles. He laced up his boots and with a hand braced on the stove, pulled himself to his feet. It took longer than he hoped to find his balance as he shuffled across the floorboards to the door.

One foot wounded, one heel gone, he whispered to himself in a sing-song chant. Take some time to find your sea legs, then you're good to go. When he reached the open door he gazed across the porch to the dry river bed and the forest beyond. Sea legs. Maybe if you'd signed up for the Navy, life would be different now. For one thing, you'd never have met Skipper. That would've changed everything.

But because of his hand, the Navy wouldn't take him. Back in the day if you wanted to taste some front-line action, the only option you could find was with a private security contractor. Like Southbridge Services Group which was assigned to bolster the offense in Afghanistan. In SSG he'd encountered Skipper. And through Skip, he found Jasper. So all in all — but mostly for the hookup with Jasper, he assured himself — he'd scored a big win.

He stood for a moment to examine the Sunday morning sunshine slipping through the tree limbs. He tugged his ball cap low over his forehead, unscrewed the bottle cap, and drank off half the ration of water. He clasped one of the twin bed rails in his hand and crossed the porch to the first step. He stood a moment to examine the ground. How had he missed it? The bear trap sprung wide open, the steel teeth bare and sharp. And beyond it, what looked like another. And over there, another. Each covered with thin layers of branches, leaves, and dry sticks.

Stepping around them, he worked his way down to the narrow trail that ran alongside the river. He turned right and, walking in a more steady gait, he pushed forward until he saw the big rock sitting in the middle of the dry river bed. What the hell was a rock like that doing here? Size of a Cadillac. He let the question go and concentrated on crossing over the stones and rocks to the north side of the creek. Fifty feet along the bank he spotted a little cove that led into the forest. Yes, this was the way. He limped to the opening, finding a rhythm of sorts, humming along as he went.

One foot wounded
One heel gone.

Chapter Twenty-One

As she walked through the forest, Eve found herself second-guessing every decision she'd made since her escape from the resort. If she'd continued her run along the road into Mendocino, by now she'd have alerted the cops and the FBI would be on the scene. Helicopters would be airborne, a SWAT team dispatched, the terrorists subdued. Or dead.

But when she saw Claws driving the Hummer along the road she made her first miscalculation. She should have hidden in the bush, waited for him to pass, then pressed on. Cutting through the forest to the river was a catastrophic error. Sure, meeting Brittany provided some relief and an alliance that helped to win the battle against Claws, but Brit's medical emergency hijacked Eve's mission. Furthermore, she imagined they could hike out to the road, commandeer the Hummer, and race into town. Another disastrous choice.

Now she found herself coaching Brit along as her friend battled the first symptoms of a pending insulin crash. Last night Brit had described the eerie manifestations that might lead to her collapse. She was known as a "brittle diabetic" and without her meds, she could experience thirst, frequent urination, mood changes. Her facial appearance could change. A pall of fear might mask her face. Her eyes might take on a glassy sheen.

"Just follow my lead," Eve said in a breezy voice to hurry them along. She checked her watch. Sunday, 8:22 AM.

"Yeah, yeah," Brit mumbled as she set one foot ahead of the other. She took another sip of juice and carefully sealed the bottle cap in place.

With the compass in hand, Eve was able to navigate their way through the forest. She knew they were on track and if she could keep Brit marching along behind her, she calculated that they'd reach the Hummer soon. She just had to keep dishing out large dollops of hope.

"First, we're going to drive the Hummer straight past the resort and down to your cabin. Then we'll get your meds. That's first."

"Yeah, yeah." She placed her hands together as if she were about to pray.

But Eve knew her plan brought up new challenges. How could she drive the Hummer past the watchful eyes of Skipper, Jasper, and Dogboy? Deal with that when the time comes, she told herself and pushed forward.

"Uh-o, uh-o" Brittany came to a halt. "Gotta pee. I gotta pee!"

Eve swung around. "Hey. Course you do. Look, squat down right here. Behind the tree, okay. There's no one else here.

"Keep an eye out?"

"Of course. Yeah, I'll keep an eye out for us." Her lips curled in a frown. Another delay. "Maybe I should pee, too."

After they relieved themselves, Brittany ate a handful of raisins and Eve took a compass bearing and checked her watch. "Another half hour and we should be there, okay?"

"Okay. I think I can make it."

Eve watched as Brittany steepled her hands again. As she led the way toward the gravel road, she heard Brittany repeating a prayer over and over again. It took another ten minutes before she could decipher the murmuring. As the trees ahead began to thin, just as the roadway came into view, she understood Brittany's chant.

"Hail Mary full of grace, the Lord is with thee, blessed art thou amongst women."

CHAPTER TWENTY-TWO

SKIPPER DRIFTED INTO a long silence as he wandered through the west side of the lodge. The restaurant was styled in the manner of late 1890's rustic elegance. The sort of place big-name bankers and profiteers would have visited, their pockets full of speculative winnings. The Carnegies and Rockefellers. The log cabin walls were decorated with black-and-white portraits of the good times in old San Francisco. Bigwigs riding in open carriages pulled by teams of horses and driven by freed slaves dressed in jockey costumes. Women in big hats waving at one another. Packed opera houses with who knows what playing on stage by who knows who. All of them long gone. Dead as dust.

He paused to study the proud image of William Randolph Hearst standing next to a statue of a naked woman inside his castle. Looks like Marilyn Monroe, he thought. Skipper knew the story of his granddaughter, Patricia Hearst. She'd seen the light. Joined up with the revolutionaries of her day. The Symbionese Liberation Army. They played their hand and died in a shoot-out. Everyone except Hearst's daughter. Someone had arranged Patty's departure before the slaughter began.

Skipper turned his lips in a sneer. That wouldn't happen to him. Today was Sunday. He checked the face of the grandfather clock ticking away next to the waiters' station. 9:47. He ran the math through his head. The team would decamp Monday at 0200, in just under sixteen hours. Although the scum were completely pacified now — the sound of Jasper firing two bullets into Finch's skull provided the shock they needed — some final arrangements were required. The words reminded him of Adolf Hitler's answer to the problems he faced back in his day. A final solution.

Skipper walked from the dining room into the lounge. The room was furnished with over twenty tables surrounded by plush easy chairs. At the far end, opposite the expansive bar, stood three pool tables, two dart boards, and a large card table littered with hundreds of jigsaw puzzle pieces. The walls were decorated with stuffed animal heads — bears, wolves, elk, raccoons, mountain lions, big horn sheep, a wolverine — all mounted on wood plaques that hung about seven feet off the floor. Just out of reach of any enviros who might want to rip them off the walls in retaliation for crimes against nature. The idea made him chuckle.

His footfalls creaked on the uneven floorboards as he crossed the room to the kitchen. He opened the swing door and watched Jasper finish up the morning routine.

"Breakfast all wrapped up?"

"Yup," she muttered without looking at him.

"You have enough eggs?"

"The place is stocked. **Finnegan** said they had over two hundred meals planned." She turned her wrist toward the exit door. "Plus there's an outdoor pantry."

He could tell by the sound of her voice that she hated him. She was only making conversation so she wouldn't have to ask him about Claws. Or calling the mission off right now.

"You give in to any special requests? Shucked oysters? Caviar?"

Another feeble joke, she thought and turned away from the dishes stacked on the counter to look at him. "Uh, no" — *you creep* — "just scrambled eggs, two toast, coffee. Like you ordered, Skipper."

When he saw the hate in her eyes, he nodded. "Did you set any aside for me?"

Her chin tipped toward the stove. "It's warming under the metal cover. Whenever you're ready for it."

"Okay. Forget the dishes. This'll be their last meal, so leave everything as is. Then get back to the Rotunda with Dogboy. Now that they've eaten, the scum will want to hit the latrine. You wrangle the girls, then keep watch while he handles the men."

She stood in silence for a moment, pondering how things might play out over the rest of the day. His face, even without the mask, didn't reveal much. The scar on his cheek had merged with the other creases on his mug. Together they set his entire character. A cold brew of anger, bitterness, loneliness.

"When you've done the latrine duty, come back here for new orders."

When she didn't respond, he said, "You got that, Jasper?"

She blinked. "Yeah. Copy that, Skipper." She turned on her heels, walked past him, pushed through swinging doors into the lobby, and back into the Rotunda.

Skipper set his breakfast plate and coffee mug on the dining room table under the portrait of William Randolph Hearst. What would the old tyrant think if he could see Skipper Jarvis feasting on eggs and Canadian bacon right now?

He swallowed a rind of bacon and turned his mind to what lay ahead. And what lay in the past. He recalled the days in Kandahār province, just along the Pakistani border. Politically a no man's land, but very much the military heart of the war. Which is why a private paramilitary brigade — Southbridge Services Group — was hired to restore order in the sector. Even today, few people understand the role that military con-tractors played in the war. All off-book, of course. SSG is where he teamed up with Hammer and Butch, his buddies on Task Force Destiny. Hammer, six-two, and obsessed with eating raw eggs every morning. He whisked three raw eggs into his coffee mug, added a shot of Tabasco sauce, and drank them down in a gulp. What a dude!

He smiled as he pushed some scrambled eggs on a wedge of toast and forked it into his mouth. If they could see him now, they'd cough up an effin' laugh. Like the old days when the three of them duped twenty-three Taliban into surrendering at the end of a box canyon. Then they realized they had a problem like they'd never confronted before.

They tied the T-men up with wrist straps and let their col-lective shame wash through them during the night. Captured by infidels in their own land. Death was preferable.

It was Hammer who proposed taking them out first thing in the morning. "No way we can troop them back to base without being ambushed ourselves."

"Hammer's right. It's dead simple." Butch swiveled his hand back and forth in the air as he eyed Skipper. "Them or us."

Skipper took a moment to consider the options. In the end, he had to agree. "On one condition." He swallowed the last scrap of rations from his kit and pointed his fork to each man in turn. "We never speak of it. Not to you. Not to me. Not to no one. If word ever gets out … "

He knew he didn't have to say anything more. Butch and Hammer nodded their silent agreement. Their pact was sealed.

Looking back now, Skipper wondered if he felt any remorse. If any of them did. He shook his head. It was war. Guilt was never part of the equation for him. It never troubled him. Same with the scum hunkered down in the Rotunda.

After they'd packed their gear and checked their weapons, the three men walked across the open track to the dirt pan where the twenty-three captives squatted together. The plan was to stand ten feet apart facing the T-men and let loose with their M16 assault rifles. One clip each, Butch figured. Maybe two if some of them lingered.

But something in the man nearest Skipper caught his eye. Somehow he'd freed himself from the plastic cuffs. Before he knew it, the young Tali leaped up and slashed a short kirpan knife across Skipper's cheek and down toward his throat. Fortunately, he'd held the curved blade backward and Skipper stumbled before the knife tore open his carotid artery. A second later Hammer cut the boy down with his M16. In less than a minute all the prisoners lay dead.

Butch quickly bound Skipper's wound. The cut to his face was nasty but not deep enough to require surgery. By the time they limped back to base camp, the men had concocted a cover story to account for his injury.

A rogue T-man had taken his chances and caught Skipper unaware. Skipper had won the skirmish and had the scar to prove it. The story made for good cheer around the camp, and over the next two weeks, most of the team in SSG ponied up a Heineken for Skipper. "A knife fight like that takes balls," the camp cook, Whiskey Jack Andrews, said, "And Skipper, you got one hairy pair."

As he swallowed the last of his coffee he knew he'd made his decision. If the team were to make an early break before sunset, the scum would have to go. And if they were going down, it would have to be done clean. No mistakes. Not like in Kandahār.

He pushed his dishes to the edge of the table and sat in contemplation. A gust of wind stirred the dust in the parking lot. Above, a thin layer of clouds swept in from the Pacific. He could feel a fall chill in the air. Better to break the team into three units, he decided. Commandeer two vehicles, one for Dogboy, the other for Jasper. One more for Claws, if he magically reappeared. But he'd take the Hummer for himself. Then send one of them south on the coast road, the other north. He'd take the dirt roads through the mountains and onto the I-5. A clean break. Job done, he'd make the bank etransfers on Monday. Fifty grand to each of them, plus Claws's share if he failed to show. As agreed. Arguments and deceptions about money always poisoned the well.

The only deception was one the team would never know. First Freedom Corps was little more than a mirage. Nothing more than a digital wallet. Two months ago someone calling himself Rupert Q reached out to him from the dark web. Q offered a million bucks to fund the operation. Five hundred K on deposit, the other five on completion. Money enough for weapons, tactical gear, the Hummer, the payout. And a bonus for Skipper himself when the mission wrapped up. Obviously, Q had deep pockets and the sort of values that Skipper admired. He knew Claws, Dogboy and Jasper would climb on board. The money alone would cinch the deal. But the prospect of taking down the fancy-ass media scum? That was the icing on the cake. And all of it wrapped up with the promise that no one would get hurt. The idea made him snigger. What did the pros say? No pain, no gain. True that.

A little before noon, Jasper returned to the dining room. The break did nothing to soften her look of contempt.

"Everything under control?"

"I guess." She ambled across the floor toward him. "They're just a bunch of cows. Chewing their cud. Waiting for what? They don't know."

He nodded. "Soft. That's the way we want 'em."

She shuffled a foot across the floor. "Skipper, what did you mean when you said breakfast was their last meal?"

His eyes narrowed. A new hint of insubordination had slipped into her voice. He decided to let it go. Indulge her. Besides, this afternoon he'd need her and Dogboy onside.

More than ever.

"Tell me, Jasper. What's your assessment of the mission right now?

She tugged off her mask. "My assessment?" Her eyebrows arched. "You looking for an honest answer?"

"Nothing less."

She glanced past him, through the window, paused, and turned back to face him. "We've had two *women* escape" — she added emphasis to assign a shameful tone — "and the squad is a man down." She hesitated, thinking she should name him. Claws. But that might diminish her assessment. Make it overly personal in Skipper's view. "Plus one of the scum, *Finch*" — this time the name counted somehow — "is fucking dead." She drew a breath. "Which is contrary to our rules of engagement ordered by First Freedom Corps. At least that's what you told us, Skipper. On day one, before any of us signed up for this mission."

Skipper absorbed all this with a look of equanimity. "I would agree. Given all that, what would you suggest we do? Under the circumstances."

She shook her head with a look of disbelief. Something had changed. What? "Under the circumstances," she repeated, "I think we should pull out of here ASAP."

"ASAP?" he chuckled and stood up from the table. "Well, well. Turns out we're in total agreement, Jasper. Which is why I said that breakfast was their last meal." He ran a hand over the scar on his jaw. "But we can't just walk down the road to the Hummer and drive off. It's basic tactics. We have to secure our retreat."

She nodded. "At the very least."

"So here are your new orders. Head back to the Hummer. Check the trunk box. Grab all the zip ties and bring them back here to the lodge. We'll tie the scum down as soon as you return."

Her lips scrunched together in a frown, then eased into a wary smile. Everything should be good now. Except for Claws. If necessary she'd keep to the original schedule and wait for him until Monday morning at 0200.

"Copy that," she said and pulled on her mask.

"Meanwhile I'll go back to the Rotunda. Give Dogboy an update and spell him off so he can prepare."

Chapter Twenty-Three

The Hummer was hidden behind a service garage in the maintenance yard about a mile west of the Big River Lodge. Jasper suspected that most people would miss the narrow fork off the road as they drove along the gravel track to the resort. Which meant it was the ideal place to hide the vehicle until early Monday morning. The operation called for three nights and two days in between. They'd planned every detail down to the duct tape and zip ties. On paper, it looked perfect.

That's the one thing Skipper got right, she told herself as she began to walk from the lodge to the Hummer. The Tinker Tank, as Claws called it. Parking the vehicle out of sight where no one would think to look for trouble. That was smart. Yeah, Skipper could be smart when it came to tactics like that. But dumb as a hammer for being too stubborn. A first strike was never enough for him. The drama only ended when his rage boiled over. And she could feel it bubbling up again. Skipper had turned the heat up too high. His order to kill Finch proved it.

What the hell is he thinking? Putting that creep Finch down. The mission was to scare the shit out of the scum. Operation Scum Scrub is what Claws called it. Well, we'd done that. Who could say we hadn't? All thirty of them huddled in a mass, squattin' in the dome hungry and tired — some of them beat up — while Dogboy shows the video of them at work, their kids playing at home. All of them crying. Not a one — not a single one of the scum — could stop their crying when they knew we had 'em all by the balls. They knew the revolution had begun. For real. And unless they changed their tune, they'd be the first to fall.

What we shoulda done — *what the original plan was* — was to squeeze 'em tight, then disappear. Show them the viddy and in the middle of Saturday night, slip out one by one when they're totally dazed and confused. Then trek back to the Hummer, drive out to the highway and into the mountains. Poof. A disappearing act like no one ever saw before.

Now she had to figure another way out. If Claws was here right now, they'd be gone yesterday. The two of them. Skip told Finch that Claws had killed Eve Noon along with that valley girl, Brittany Swank. That was the first Jasper heard of it. And it was prob'ly true. No one had ever out-played Claws, 'specially out in the wild. Bears, mountain lions, snakes. None of them could out-fox him. Mostly because he was a wildman himself. Like Mama always said, takes one to know one.

Yeah, after today it'll be just me and Claws. She shook her head and smiled.

His real name was Frank Jurgonski. When they first started to roll together, one night in bed when he told her his name, she called him Frankie. She liked that. Reminded her of the song Frankie and Johnnie. Except Frankie was the girl and Jasper liked that, too. A girl with a boy's name.

But Claws wouldn't hear it. "Nope, don't call me that."

"No? Why not? It's from a real sweet song."

"Frankie? It's fuckin' gay. 'Less you're sayin' I'm gay." A tinge of disrespect hung in his voice.

"Ha-ha! No, I'm not saying that, honey." She felt down between his legs and he let out a little sigh of delight. Something almost gentle.

"No. Just call me *Claws*. Everyone calls me that."

She paused a moment. She wanted to ask him how it happened. But how to say it without prying?

While he waited for her to speak, he ran the stubs of his amputated fingers over her face.

She took this as a sign to continue her explorations. "So you don't mind people saying that about your fingers?"

"No." He coughed up a chuckle. "My pop told me to make the best outta what I've got. Kids at school called me Claws — as if they feared me."

His voice was hard. Proud.

"So ... how'd it happen?"

"You really want to know?"

"Only if you want to tell it."

He nodded, looked away, then a moment later turned back to her. "At my Uncle Jeb's cabin. When I was a kid, just eight. We were visiting him in Tennessee. He had this backwoods shack where he was building stuff. Making boards out of raw logs. I watched him and Pop cutting shingles with a rusty old chop saw. End of the day when Pop and Uncle Jeb were drinking on the back porch, I started up the saw. Somehow … I dunno … I reached over to grab a stick of wood. At the same time, the blade came down on my hand." He looked at her and blinked. "It was done before I knew it."

"Sweet lord. That must of been — "

"No, none of that." He held up his hand to stop her from saying any more. "This hand works just fine."

"I know. I've seen you do stuff. Like everything that needs doing gets done."

"True enough. Besides, it makes me feel like a tiger."

"A tiger?" She laughed. "You *are* a tiger. *A tiger man.* I never met anyone like you."

"Rrrrrr." His throat rumbled and the sound emerged as a heavy purr. Then he caressed her face with the stubs of his hand. And when he continued to fondle her breasts and hip and down into the center of her world, she felt herself collapse into him.

No matter how long it took, she would be his. And he would be hers alone.

Chapter Twenty-Four

"Okay, Brit. We're here." She held a finger to her closed lips. "Let's be quiet now. We'll cross here and find the service road, okay?"

A look of shock crossed her face. "We're here?"

"Almost." To her surprise, she saw what looked like a fork in the road just fifty yards ahead.

The service road was little more than two parallel dirt tracks compacted into hardpan ruts from years of vehicles traversing through the heavily wooded valley that sloped north toward Pudding Creek. As she led the way along the furrow on the left, Eve slipped Claws's AR-15 from her shoulder. When they'd left the burnt-out cabin she'd decided it was better to unburden Brittany and carry both weapons herself. No telling what they might encounter, she told herself. Perhaps a fifth terrorist had been assigned to guard the Hummer. The thought made her stomach churn and she turned to Brittany who lagged behind her, shuffling along in a daze. Eve knew she had to get her friend to the Redwood cottage within the next hour to find her insulin supplies.

"Hey, Brit. You okay?"

A nod.

"Good. So let's cut into the trees here. Just to be safe."

She waited for Brittany to catch up, then tugged her by the elbow into the woods and found a way through the low salal. They walked slowly until she spotted three sheds standing in a row. She took a moment to examine them. All three were single-story buildings constructed from rough-cut cedar. The roofs were clad in corrugated steel. Each had identical double doors secured with heavy-duty padlocks. Opaque glass windows on the right and left of the buildings' doors had steel bars bolted to the frames to protect the glass. All three outbuildings looked impregnable and she couldn't detect any breaches to the windows, doors, or rooflines.

But where was the Hummer?

"Come on," she whispered, drawing Brittany along until they stood side-on to the shed closest to the forest.

And there it was. A black 2010 Hummer H3. Parked parallel to the back of the middle shed, well hidden from anyone who might drive up the rutted track. The vehicle was the five-door model with a spare tire mounted on the trunk. Eve recognized it after Gabe Finkleman, her research assistant at *The Post*, took her on a spin through the Berkeley Hills after he purchased an identical H3 last year.

Then she spotted a flicker of movement at the rear of the vehicle. The trunk door swung to the side and seemed to lock into place. Someone gathering supplies. Then she noticed a desert camo shirt as the prowler reached into the cab for something. Jasper — on her own and without a mask.

Eve took a backward step to hide behind a tree trunk. She nodded to herself as she watched Jasper gather supplies, some food, and a clutch of zip ties. As Jasper busied herself at the truck, a new thought came to Eve. Yes, she murmured to herself. It could work. This could solve everything.

She turned to study Brittany for a moment. It was obvious that she had no fight left in her. Eve would have to confront Jasper on her own. She held a finger to her lips and waited until Brittany nodded an acknowledgment. They had to operate in complete silence. Eve mouthed two words: *Dead silence.* Again Brittany nodded. Although she hadn't seen Jasper, she seemed to grasp the gravity of the situation.

Eve unbuttoned the top of her shirt. Then she pointed to Brittany and mouthed the words, *You too.* Brittany shrugged, and whispered, "What?" Eve shook her head to silence her, then she began to unbutton her friend's shirt. She smiled as she worked her way down the row of buttons. Her face suggested that this is a game. A lark. Brittany put on a feeble grin as if she understood. She knew that a plan of some kind was underway and she let Eve continue to undress her. Then Eve unbuckled the belt and slipped off Brittany's pants and shoes. Brittany's face swam with an expression of confusion.

Eve guided her to a tall sugar pine tree and helped her to sit down and lean against the tree trunk. She uncapped the juice bottle and made a motion for her to take a drink. She did. Then Eve took the bottle from her and tucked it between Brittany's bare, outstretched legs. Only a sip or two remained. She looked into her eyes, pressed her finger to her lips again, and whispered one word. "Wait."

Then she gathered Brittany's clothes under her left arm and made her way back to the blind where she'd observed Jasper. When Eve watched her swing around the front of the Hummer, Eve dropped the clothing to the ground. She gripped the hand-guard of the rifle in her left hand and braced the stock of the AR-15 against her right shoulder. Her right finger hovered over the trigger guard. She drew a breath. Exhaled. Then sucked one long gulp of air into her lungs.

"Jasper! Step away from the Hummer and lie on the ground!"

Jasper turned toward Eve. Her jaw dropped open. Her left foot took a step forward but then she froze. Her mouth wobbled as if she wanted to shout, then it locked tight in a bleak frown.

"Make no mistake, Jasper. I'm an ex-cop. I know what I'm doing. *I'm not fucking around.*" She stepped toward the back of the closest shed and continued to approach Jasper at a steady, even pace. "And in case you're wondering, I took a man down before. More than once."

Jasper's eyes fluttered as she recognized Eve. Yeah, she'd been a cop. She'd seen her profile. Decorated. Promoted. Jasper realized that she'd been ambushed by a pro. But maybe they could negotiate. She'd saved Finch's life. That had to count for something.

"Look. Things at the lodge changed since yesterday."

"Doesn't matter." Eve waved the AR-15 at Jasper's feet. "Face down on the ground."

As she slumped onto her knees, Jasper waved a hand. "Look, I saved your husband's life. He'd be dead without me."

The words sent a chill through her arms. How bad did it get in the Rotunda? She steadied her hands on the weapon. "Just get down."

Jasper slumped on her belly. She turned her head to one side so that she could speak. "Look. Don't shoot me. I know where Finch is. He's tied up where Skipper can't find him."

"What're you saying?"

"He's in the forest. Without me, you'll never find him. *I fuckin' put him there.*"

Something in Jasper's voice made Eve hesitate. But she knew she had to move forward. First things first. Her teeth ground together and she pointed the AR-15 at Jasper's face. "No more talking. Now take your clothes off."

"What?" Her voice trembled with disbelief.

"Stay on your belly. Boots first. Then your combat fatigues."

"What?"

"Now!"

Jasper reached under her legs and struggled to take off her right boot. Then her left.

"Toss 'em over."

She threw the boots toward the shed.

"Now the pants and shirt. The balaclava too."

Lying face down, it took a moment for her to strip off her shirt and pants. When her clothes were set aside, Eve called into the woods.

"Brit, you can come out now."

No reply. Eve tightened her grip on her weapon. She didn't want to leave Jasper on her own while she dragged Brittany to the Hummer.

"Brit! You hear me?"

"Yes." A whimper.

"Good. Everything's good out here. Come on out. We're going to get your meds, okay?"

Wearing a bra, underpants, and socks, Brittany stumbled into the yard and stepped toward the first shed. She paused a moment to assess the scene before her.

Eve waved her hand to redirect her. "Brit, look behind you. I put your clothes on the ground. Bring 'em over here."

Brittany noticed the pile of discarded clothing next to Jasper. The look on her face revealed that she understood some kind of plan that Eve had concocted. But what could she be thinking? She gathered her clothes and brought them to Eve.

"Who's this?" She leaned over to study the prisoner.

"Jasper."

"Who?"

Eve realized that aside from Claws, Brittany hadn't encountered any of the terrorists. "One of the cammies," she said. "Look, put on her clothes, okay? You're about the same size as her. You have to drive the Hummer down to the resort in her clothes." When she saw Brittany's blank expression, she dangled Jasper's balaclava in her hand. "Don't worry, with the mask over your face, they'll think you're her."

Brittany nodded. "Okay, I get it. Just so you know, I just finished the last of the juice."

"Okay. We'll go as soon as you're dressed."

A faint smile crossed her lips after she'd dressed in Jasper's combat fatigues. "Jeez, they fit."

"I thought they might. Now tie on the boots."

Boots on, Brittany stood next to Eve.

"One more thing. Put on the mask." She passed her the balaclava. "Just in case some of the other cammies show up."

Brittany tugged on the mask. For a moment Eve wondered if this was the right move. She couldn't see her friend's face and had no visual indication if she was slipping into insulin shock. On the other hand, the mask would be necessary when the Hummer pulled into the resort. Better to get Brittany used to it now.

"Okay, now listen. This is important. We're going to put your clothes on Jasper. Can you keep the rifle on her?"

"What for?" She pointed at the Hummer, "Let's leave her here and go."

Eve shook her head. "She's the only one who knows where Will is."

"Will's missing?"

Jasper rolled her head toward Brittany. "Fuckin' right. Tied up tight. Without me, he'll die of thirst."

Brittany snarled. "Just like Claws. That's how we left him."

"What?" Jasper barked.

When she realized that Brittany had let the cat out of the bag, Eve was quick to respond. "Don't worry, we left him with enough water for two days."

"Fuck you!" Jasper barked.

"Listen, you get me to Will and I'll get you to Claws. A one-for-one trade."

"Fuck!" Jasper shouted in disbelief.

"Shut up," Eve whispered, her voice brittle with determination, "or I'll end you right now." She glared at Brittany. "And not another word from you, either."

Her head tipped forward in a slight nod. Even with the mask covering her face, Eve could detect Brittany's sheepishness.

"Brit, this is *it*. Showtime. Are you ready for this?"

"Yeah." Her hand reached out to take the AR-15.

Eve waved her free hand to ward off any rash moves. "Look, this thing can fire off fifteen rounds in seconds. So keep your fingers on the trigger guard. *Not on the trigger itself.* And point the muzzle at her feet."

Brittany drew a breath. "Got it."

"All right. Stand over there." She pointed to a spot about five feet away next to the back of the middle shed. When Brittany was in position, Eve said, "Do *not* fire unless I tell you to, okay?"

Brittany nodded and looked down at her prisoner. Eve drew the Sig26 from its holster and pointed it at Jasper's spine.

"This is your one chance to earn your freedom, Jasper. Like I said, I do *not* want to shoot you." She took a moment to reassure herself that the next step in her plan would work. "Now stand up and put on Brit's clothes."

Jasper struggled to her feet. She wiped a smudge of dirt from her face and brushed some dried twigs from her belly and legs. She glanced at Eve and Brittany, studying the weapons pointed at her. She stared at Eve while she tipped her chin toward Brittany.

"Jesus. She doesn't know what she's doing with the 15."

"All the more reason for you to follow orders."

She began to pull on Brittany's clothing. When she was dressed she shook her head with a look of despair. "Now what?"

"The zip ties. I saw you with them. Where'd you put them?"

"Shotgun." Her chin nudged toward the front passenger seat.

Eve gathered the batch of ties from the truck. They were snugged together by a single twist-tie. She carried them back to Jasper.

"Brit, pay attention while I strap her wrists."

"On it." She ran her left hand along the ridged stock of the handguard surrounding the gun barrel, then slid it back so that the V in her elbow flexed into a comfortable position. She was ready to fire.

Eve slipped the Sig26 into her holster and pulled one zip tie loose from the bundle. She dropped the rest to the ground. "Hands out front," she said and stepped toward Jasper.

With her eyes fixed on Eve's face, Jasper eased her hands forward, fists clumped together. When she saw Eve turn her attention to the zip tie, Jasper swung both arms above her right shoulder and smashed her bunched fists into the left side of Eve's head. The blow drove her onto her knees. Wobbling to recover her balance, she braced her right hand on the dirt. As she teetered there Jasper drew her right foot back and planted a round-house kick into Eve's ribs. The blow sent her sprawling to the ground. With the wind knocked out of her, she gasped for breath and pulled her arms to her chest.

Jasper then turned to Brittany. She shook her head from

side to side, a gesture that said, *Sorry girl, you're next.* "Hand me the 15 or I'll put you down for good."

Brittany shuddered. She could feel her stomach swimming as if she was about to discharge her guts in one vast, horrible explosion. Tears rolled down her cheeks and clotted the face mask as she sobbed in long, jagged whimpers. The AR-15 clattered as she dropped the weapon at her feet.

As Jasper stooped to pick up the rifle she took another look at Eve. Good. Down for the count, she told herself. She pointed the rifle at Brittany and rotated the muzzle in a circling motion. "Turn round."

Brittany's arms began to tremble. Did someone say to turn around? She pirouetted on her toes and turned until she faced the Hummer's passenger door.

Something about the woman seemed off. Jasper scratched the back of her head. "What's wrong with you?"

"Nothing," she muttered, then added, "much."

"You know where Claws is?" She shoved the barrel of the rifle into the middle of Brittany's back.

"Uh-huh."

"Get in the truck. I'll drive, you show me where to find him."

Chapter Twenty-Five

CLAWS CONTINUED TO chant his mantra as he trudged through the forest. He held a steel bed rail in one hand and punched it into the dirt as he plodded along. Each strike provided a kind of percussion beat — BAM — to the end of each phrase.

One foot wounded
One heel gone.
BAM.

After he'd left the big rock in the river and turned into the forest, it didn't take him long to adopt a marching tempo. He knew that after an hour or so he'd be able to rise above the pain in his foot. And by keeping the forest shade to his left, he sensed his bearing would hold a northbound direction.

But his determination wasn't limited to finding his way back to the Hummer. Or to take out the two chickadees who'd outmaneuvered him back at the shack. No, the whole mission had to be scrapped. Skipper had totally blown them off course. They were only supposed to scare the shit outta the media clowns. Operation Scum Scrub.

He knew Jasper would agree. And last month, the minute he laid eyes on her he knew the two of them would pair off. Dogboy and Skip could join them if they wanted for the first leg out of the forest, but he and Jasper were driving the Tinker Tank outta the bush into the mountains where his brother had built his End-of-the-World hideaway. EOW, he called it as his voice rose in a weird screech of defiance. He'd put away a year's supply of food and ammo, all stowed away tight as a drum. Waterproof. Bulletproof. Cop proof. God-proof if it came to it. No way would he bring Skip and Dogboy along with him and Jasper to EOW. The other two could jump ship anywhere along the line. Mendocino. Or up the coast in some Dogpatch village. Who cares? Just dump 'em and run.

Yes, it would be just him and Jasper. Or Jasmine — her real name. Jasmine Winters, she told him that night in Frisco. He liked the Jasmine part. The way she smelled like a bed of flowers lying in his arms. But Winters? No way, the girl was hot. Bull hot. Hotter than anyone he'd met. Even the pros in Mexico. But when he called her Jasmine, she wouldn't have it. "Jasper," she insisted. "My actual middle name. And it's the name of a big beautiful park up in Canada."

He said they should go there one day. She smiled at that. "You mean together? Just us?"

"Yeah. Jasper and Jasper. It'd be like havin' two of you."

He remembered the soft tug of her laughter as he brushed some sweat from his forehead and paused to drink another slug of water.

The memory of the beautiful glow on her face made him laugh, too. But what he recalled now was the laughter of stupidity. The stupidity of the other women. Nice of the two chickadees to leave him with a bit of drink. But totally amateur hour. They had no idea. In war, it's either kill or be killed. And when he saw them next, they would die.

He looked into the treetops and tried to assess the slope of the shadows. Not much showing. Which means midday. Which also means you are getting close to the road. And the Tinker Tank.

Ten minutes later a smile dawned on his soiled face. The shrubs thinned out and opened onto the road. He stood a moment to find his bearings. Turn left or right to get to the service road? He must've driven up and down this stretch five times two nights ago. Then he noticed the towering redwood tree up to his left. Yeah, that's the one that made him wonder about the sound it would make when it toppled over. *BOOM!*

He turned left and continued along the road until he reached the twin tire tracks of the road that led up to the Hummer. He could feel his heartbeat accelerate. Adrenaline thrummed in his arms and legs. He shuffled along the track until he saw the three cedar sheds ahead. Finally. He slowed to a steady walk and approached the middle shed, his mind unable to release the chant that had accompanied him this far.

One foot wounded
One heel gone.
BAM.

When he reached the rear corner of the building he came to an abrupt halt. What was this? *Fuck.* The tall one sprawled on the ground, choking for air. And the other pointing an AR-15 at Jasper's back. *The fuckin' chickadees.* He held his breath and stepped back behind the sidewall of the shed. Think. *Think!* He knew what would happen if the girl slipped up. If she fired the 15, Jasper would be cut down. Damn it. Knowing what had to be done — what he had to do right now — he nodded to himself. You've got one move only. He gripped the steel bar in both hands and raised it over his shoulder. He glanced around the corner and measured the distance to the girl holding the rifle. Five steps, maybe six if his foot stumbled. Just five steps but you move with stealth. No wind. He drew a breath, let it out. Another. Then a third — and held it.

He rounded the corner and counted his strides. Two, three, four. *Now.* He swung the steel rail up and around, then down hard as he could into the head of the chickadee. As the impact juddered the rail through his arms he heard her skull crack open. A light spray of blood dashed through the air and she toppled to the ground.

"Fuckin' over!" he screamed and leaned over to watch the death throes of the woman convulsing in the dirt at his feet.

He stared at the body below him, glanced away, then back again. *What?* First, came the shock of recognition, then the horror welling through his belly as he absorbed what he'd done. He dropped the steel rail and fell to his knees. His hands cupped Jasper's face, her ears, the back of her head — as if he could somehow patch the pieces of her skull together and seal them in place. Her blood drizzled over his fingers, the amputated fingers unable to contain the life draining from the only woman who had ever offered him her love. Her body. Her heart and soul.

"No. No, no, no," he wailed. "Not this. *Not like this!"*

Eve's eyes flickered as she watched him groveling above Jasper's corpse. Finally, she could take in a lungful of air. She watched Brittany slump onto the ground and lean against the truck's front bumper. She pulled the mask from her face. Her eyes were glazed, icy.

Eve's hand slipped the pistol from the holster on her belt. No telling what happens next, she said to herself. Get ready for anything. She focused on her breathing. Counted each breath. Five, six, seven. Then she saw Claws shuffling forward on the ground. Crawling toward Brittany, his fingers tearing at the soil as he approached her.

Eve pulled herself to her knees, then stood. She clamped the Sig26 in her right hand and supported it with her left. She braced her feet in a wide stance to restore her balance.

"Claws," she muttered, her voice barely a whisper. "*Claws.* Stop right there."

He turned his head to look back at her. His lips twisted with anger.

"Do not move another inch toward her."

He propped himself on one knee. A look of recognition crossed his face. He reached out and grasped the steel rail in his left hand. *"You.* You fuckin' bitch."

He used the rail to right himself, climbed to his feet, and squared his shoulders to face Eve. A bull preparing to charge.

Eve adjusted her grip on the pistol. Her finger slipped from the trigger guard onto the trigger.

"No," she cautioned him, "not one more — "

As he rushed her, Eve fired a round point blank into his chest. Her hand shuddered with the recoil and she reset her posture. His vest had blocked a lethal kill. He stumbled and lurched forward again. She aimed for his nose and fired the handgun again and again. How many shots hit his head? Four? Six? She had no idea.

Then at last — when all her senses seemed to collide in a starburst — he fell to the ground. He toppled sideways, one arm flopped over Jasper's ankle. Eve dropped the pistol and slumped backward, reeling from the trauma. Then she heard something. A slight, wordless sputter wheezing from his lips. What was it? *Nothing,* she told herself. Nothing at all. Who can tell what the dying confess as they pass into oblivion?

CHAPTER TWENTY-SIX

LEFT IN A daze from the battle with Claws, Eve couldn't determine how long she'd stood next to the corpses behind the shed. Somehow the shock had loosened her connection to the passage of time. But when she heard Brittany call to her she came to her senses.

"Eve."

She turned her head and studied Brittany's body slouched against the Hummer's front bumper. Her cheeks appeared drained, colorless. Eve looked at Claws and Jasper. Fortunately, their faces were turned away so she couldn't see their eyes. She considered Claws's fingers with an air of detached appraisal. What was it like to go through life with your fingers chopped off like that?

"Eve?"

You have no time for this, she told herself. No time for the dead. No time to assess blame or responsibility. There was another world out there. Other people. Other needs.

"Yeah. I'm okay." She held up a finger to suggest she

needed another second or two to find her bearings. She slid the pistol into the holster on her waist.

"I'm fading."

Eve ran a hand over her friend's face. A lingering caress, soft with tenderness and compassion. The same warmth she offered her daughter when she'd come down with the flu.

"Let's see what I can find." She opened the passenger door and glanced inside the truck. At first glance, she could see it was loaded with tactical gear and electronic equipment. "Decked out" — the expression Gabe Finklemen used to describe his Hummer.

She walked to the trunk door and swung it open. A plastic tarp covered the interior contents. She tossed the tarp to the ground and kicked it aside while she studied the array of crates and supplies. Stacked against the rear seat a steel case marked AMMO was secured with a combination lock. Next to it stood a cardboard tray of ammunition for the Sig26. She drew her pistol from the holster, released the magazine, reloaded it with fifteen rounds, and slid the weapon back onto her hip. On the right side of the trunk sat a cardboard box holding a dozen plastic bottles of water. Beside that, stood a six-pack of Gatorade. A paperboard container held eight or ten packets of dried fruit. Apricots, banana chips, blueberries. Bingo. She twisted the cap off the water bottle, swallowed a long drink, then opened another bottle for Brittany.

"Here. Maybe this'll help." She held the bottle to her friend's lips and watched her take a sip. Seconds later she guzzled down a good long drink. Eve then ripped open a pack of dried berries. Brittany seized it in both hands, dumped four or five into her mouth, and began to chew them to a pulp.

"Oh my God, Eve. Thanks." For the first time since they reached the Hummer, her voice sounded hopeful.

Eve gathered the tarp in her hands and slung it over Jasper's and Claws's bodies. She took a moment to ponder their brief battle, then tucked the tarp under their torsos, legs, and heads so that the breeze coming up the valley from the ocean wouldn't unfurl the cover. Bad enough to see them die in a fit of rage at the back of a shed, but quite another to leave them exposed in the dirt where raptors would rip them apart piece by piece.

"Okay, I'm going to check the gear in the cab." Eve pointed to the driver's seat. "Meantime, drink and eat up. When you're ready, we'll drive back to your cabin and get your meds, okay?"

Brittany nodded. Her eyes now alive with fresh hope.

Eve slipped an arm around Brittany's shoulder, squeezed her in a light embrace, then climbed into the Hummer. She clutched the steering wheel in both hands as she studied the dashboard.

Given its vaunted military provenance, the interior of a Hummer H3 appeared remarkably similar to any high-end SUV. Speedometer, odometer, gear shifter, turn signals, wipers, AM-FM radio, headlamps, brake set and release. But installed above the radio set, an after-market GPS system stood at the ready. A Globalstar satellite phone.

"Yes."

She lifted the handset and studied the various settings. She'd used a sat-phone before and understood that they all sported different options. Some were designed for emergency use only, and some just for regional calls. Others provided global connections. This device didn't appear to have a selector to choose one over another. Likely the Globalstar had a preset range. Good enough to reach the Mendocino cop shop, she hoped. Or failing that, the SFPD.

She clicked the connect button and waited for the phone screen to respond. Nothing. "No," she whispered. *Impossible.* She turned the phone in her fingers, searching for other buttons or switches that might bring the phone to life. She checked the power cord to the phone. "Unplugged," she muttered. She spotted the power port just above the twin coffee cup holder and connected the phone cord. Still no response from the phone. Could it be dead? Maybe sitting idle for a full day had depleted the charge.

Then a thought struck her. *Start the engine.* She rolled down the window and called Brittany.

"Brit, I'm gonna start the truck. You ready to go?"

After a moment, Brittany swung open the passenger door and leaned over the seat. "Now?"

"Are you feeling better?"

"A little."

"Hop in," Eve said as she slipped the key into place and turned the ignition.

Thruuuummm. The guttural power of the engine filled the cab. A baritone sex bomb. She smiled and turned to Brittany. "You know, I can see why guys love this thing."

Brittany rolled her eyes with a look of complete disinterest and swallowed another long drink from the water bottle. It was half-empty now.

Eve studied the phone again. The keypad radiated an amber glow. "Oh yeah. Look, we got juice, Brit!" For the first time since she'd been dragged out of the Sugar Pine cottage, she felt a burst of optimism swell through her chest.

"Omigod." Brittany's face lit up. "Call the cops!"

"Damn right."

But how? If the Globalstar had an onboard directory, she had no idea how to find it. So, time for another Plan B. Call the San Francisco Police Department. The telephone number was seared into her memory. A sense of dread filled her as she recalled her years working for the force. She'd been emotionally wounded. Scarred by the constant sexual bullying. But the SFPD telephone number seemed to float above her right now — a life ring hovering inches from her grasp. She had to reach out and call them.

The operator answered on the second ring. "SFPD. Officer Stephanie Waters speaking. How can I direct your call?"

"Officer Waters, my name is Eve Noon. I'm an ex-SFPD officer." Eve could feel her heart pumping as she spoke. Everything now depended on how she handled this call. She remembered the necessary code to identify her call as critical. "This is a code 10-36 emergency notification. Do you get that?"

"Yes. I read you. What is your situation?"

"I'm at a remote resort thirty miles east of Mendocino off Highway One. I am one of over thirty people taken hostage by four terrorists. Shots have been fired and at least two are dead. I need to speak to your Chief of Special Operations."

"I understand, ma'am, but first I need to verify your identity." Her voice hummed with vibrant tension. "What was your badge number?"

Eve paused. "What?"

"Your SFPD badge number. What was it?

Eve rattled off the number, then added, "What's the name of the current CSO?"

She waited while Waters checked Eve's ID in the database. "All right, I have you here. The CSO is Victor Wainwright. Hang on while I put you through. It may take a moment to red-light your call. But I will get you through."

"All right." Eve exhaled a long sigh. She felt as if she were entering a gladiator ring. To calm herself she gazed through the Hummer windshield at the treetops and above them, the open sky now filling with heavy clouds. On any other day, she'd feel as if she'd been transported to Heaven. A walk through the wilderness, hand-in-hand with Will, the redwood trees towering above them.

"Chief Wainwright speaking."

"Chief, I'm Eve Noon, an ex-SFPD officer. I'm calling on a satellite phone thirty miles east of Mendocino." She repeated the details that she'd reported to Waters and asked Wainwright to respond with immediate force and effect.

"Slow down, Noon. I'm bringing up your profile on my screen. I just need to check something."

She could hear him breathing in a raspy wheeze as he scrolled through her profile. A cigarette smoker? Sounded like a two-pack-a-day man.

"Okay, got it. I knew I'd heard your name before."

She paused, unsure what her profile might reveal. "I was

the media relations officer."

"Among other things." His voice had a dismissive tone. "Look, I need to verify your ID before we go on. Waters gave your badge number. Now tell me your PIN.

She should have expected this. After winning two million dollars in an out-of-court settlement against the SFPD for sexual abuse and harassment, she'd left the force in a blaze of glory. At least as far as the women officers were concerned.

"It's B25634." The serial number tattooed on her grand-mother's arm when she was in Auschwitz-Birkenau. Eve Asimov had survived the horrors of the concentration camp and passed on her story to young Eve. Another number she'd never forget.

"Okay. You're clear. But FYI, I'm recording this call. And if this proves bogus I'll personally see that it comes back to bite you."

"It won't. Look, there are more than thirty hostages in imminent threat from two terrorists armed with AR-15s and pistols."

"The message from Waters said there were four terrorists."

"Yeah. Were. Two are down."

A pause. "Two of four terrorists are down?" His voice tone suggested a measure of respect.

"Confirmed."

The line seemed to go dead. Why was he hesitating? Eve could feel the pulse in her neck quicken.

"Chief?"

"I'm here."

"Chief, these men are desperate. The hostages are corralled

in a geodesic dome. They have no shoes, no food, no phones. Any second they could be killed."

"All right, Noon. Copy that. I've located your position through your sat-phone. I'm rolling this over to the FBI and Homeland. I've requested a chopper for immediate recon. You should see a bird above you in twenty minutes. Likely they'll airdrop a SWAT team to the ground. Is there a clear place for them to drop?"

Finally, she felt she'd earned his respect.

"Best place is where you've got me. A service yard with three sheds about a mile east of the resort. And tell them the dome is attached to the lodge office. That's where the hostages are pinned down."

"I'll pass it on."

"Thanks, Chief."

"Thank me later." His voice erupted with a rough cough. When he recovered, he continued. "Are you good to go?"

"Yes, sir."

"My advice is to drive your vehicle to safety and stay close to your phone."

"Understood, sir."

She clicked off the phone handset and peered through the window. Drive to safety? Maybe after she drove past the lodge where Skipper and Dogboy maintained a close watch. Maybe after she found her husband. A feeble laugh gurgled up Eve's throat. Right. Maybe after she had a complete nervous breakdown.

She turned to look at Brittany. Difficult to assess her fitness.

"Brit, you think you can drive?"

"What?"

"That's why you're in those clothes. So they think you're Jasper."

Brittany shrugged. "What if you put on the mask? Wouldn't that work?"

Eve shook her head. Jasper was about five-foot-four, an average woman's height. Eve was six-two. "I'm too tall."

Brittany needed a moment to mull this over. She took another gulp of water. "How far is it?"

"About a mile to the lodge. Then just along the trail to your cottage. Ten minutes from now you can get your insulin."

She let out a puff of air. "Yeah. Okay, I know it's my turn to step up."

"Good." Eve opened her door and waved a hand to Brittany. "Okay, slide over. Let's get you used to driving this thing."

CHAPTER TWENTY-SEVEN

WHOA. EVE GRIT her teeth as Brittany steered the Hummer along the parallel tire tracks of the service road. Was she capable of turning onto the main road and gliding past Skipper and Dogboy at the lodge? What about coasting down the chip trail and along the row of cabins? Watching her hands skitter back and forth on the steering wheel made Eve wonder if she should take over the driving.

"Don't panic," Brittany whispered as she reached the junction to the main road.

Eve wasn't sure if Brittany was talking to herself or trying to settle Eve's nerves. "Okay," she said to bolster her confidence.

"I used to drive a tractor on my dad's farm. I just need to figure out the turning radius on this thing." She guided the vehicle onto the asphalt road and straightened the wheels.

Turning radius, Eve mused. Obviously, she'd regained some capacity for driving.

"That's good, Brit." Eve exhaled an easy breath and examined Brittany's outfit. The camo jacket and pants, the balaclava, her posture. All of it looked convincing enough. "You know, I think we can do this."

A few minutes later, as the truck approached the signs identifying the resort, Eve ducked down in her seat. "Okay, you're on your own 'til we reach the trail to the cabins. You remember how it looks?"

"Course." Her voice sounded assured. Adopting the voice of a tour guide, she began to point out the surrounding scenery. "Check the redwoods on both sides of the road. And here's the hand-carved sign. *Big River Resort, 100 Yards.*"

For the first time since they'd joined forces at the abandoned cabin, Brittany's mood seemed elevated. Had her symptoms evaporated, or was this a final, dizzy precursor to an insulin crash? Eve could only hope for the former.

"You got this, Brit."

"Yeah. What do the kids say?" — she turned her head to the right as they swung in front of the lodge — *"frickin' A!"*

"Right. Something like that."

"We're here. There's the sign on the porch. *Guests Please Register Here.*"

Eve felt the truck slowing. "Brit, don't slow down. We want to drive down the trail to the cottages, right?"

"Don't we hav'ta check in?"

Eve felt the Hummer coast into the parking lot. Loose gravel crunched under the tires as the truck slowed to a crawl.

"Brit. Keep going."

"Where? I don't get it."

Eve dipped her head above the dash to mark her bearings.

"Straight ahead. At the far end of the parking lot. And don't turn to look into the lodge. Eyes on the road."

"Oh shit. I think he saw us."

"Who?"

"A cammie. Through the window." Her left hand came off the wheel to point at the geodesic dome.

"Don't worry about it. He'll think you're Jasper. Give the truck a little gas at the end of the parking lot."

Eve could feel the car turn slightly as it gained some momentum.

"Okay. I see what you mean now. Here's the trail. Sorry, I forgot."

"Are you out of the parking lot now?"

"Yeah. But the trail's pretty narrow."

Eve sat up and glanced at the path leading down to the row of cottages.

"No problem, Brit. This thing's made for off-road driving. Just keep the left wheel on the trail and put my side up on the shoulder here." She pointed to the right. "It's a bit bumpy. But in two minutes we'll be home free."

She nudged the Hummer up onto the shoulder. The steering wheel juddered in her hands and she let out a gasp. "No, I don't like this."

Her arms locked at the elbow as she tried to pull back into the center of the trail. Ahead to the left stood a concrete four-foot cube with a steel door. An electrical relay station that supplied power to the row of cottages.

"Brit. Slow down a little. And don't hit that box."

"I can't."

"What?"

"I can't steer anymore!" she shouted, pulling her hands away from the steering wheel and covering her face.

Eve grabbed the wheel in her left hand and tried to pull them back onto the shoulder again. Too late. The Hummer crashed into the concrete box with a heavy thud that sent a shudder through the frame. The engine cut out and a flashing light lit up the dash.

"Okay. Seat belts off." Eve unclicked Brittany's belt, then her own. "On foot, Brit. Grab your stuff, and let's go."

Eve pulled the AR-15 strap over her shoulder and stepped onto the ground. She swung open the rear truck door and stuffed her pockets with the remaining granola bars and two bottles of water. If they were lucky they'd find more sandwiches in Brittany's cottage refrigerator. As an afterthought, she slipped a dozen zip ties into her back pocket. Then she walked to the driver's door, pulled it open, and helped Brittany find her balance as she stepped out of the truck.

"You okay?"

"I dunno."

"You're in the Redwood, right?"

When Brittany didn't respond, Eve looked along the trail. The Redwood stood on the right, four doors along the chip trail. As they stepped past the electrical relay box, Eve glanced around to study the damage to the Hummer. It looked worse than she imagined. The corner of the concrete box had crimped the front bumper into a sharp V just below the hood. The impact had driven something into the engine. A spray of gray vapor hissed across the windshield.

"Come on." She guided Brittany along by her elbow. When they reached the Redwood, Eve turned the front door handle. It opened and the door swung into the room. She glanced around the cottage. Either Brittany was an appalling housekeeper, or someone had ransacked the cabin.

"We made it." She pulled her friend into a celebratory hug. "Brit, where's your insulin supply?"

Again, no reply. Her hand, visibly shaking, pointed to the refrigerator.

Eve opened the mini-fridge. On the top rack, a glass vial lay on its side. Eve read the label which identified Brittany's name, medication code number and name, and an expiry date.

"Brittany, look." She lifted one vial in her hand. "Do you know what to do with this?"

Brittany's eyes widened, the pupils dilating as she examined the medication. She nodded once and clasped the vial in her fingers. "Syringe," she muttered and cast her eyes on her backpack. "Inside."

Eve opened the pack and found the insulin kit in a rigid leather case. She opened the flap and saw the syringe and the empty insulin vial — drained from Brittany's last dose. As she turned back to her friend, Eve lifted the needle in her hand. "Here."

"Fix," she whispered, tilting her head in a lazy nod.

"Jeez, Brit, I don't — "

"Fix!" She shoved the vial into Eve's hand and tugged up her camo shirt exposing her belly.

Eve blinked as she summoned the strength to prep a shot. Years ago she'd trained to administer injections in an emergency, but she'd never been called upon to actually apply her vague understanding of the procedure. Now's the time, she told herself. Most important, she thought, was to draw the exact dosage of insulin into the syringe. Back at the big rock, Brittany said twenty-eight units. She plunged the needle tip through the vial seal and pulled the plunger up to the prescribed level. When the insulin hit the twenty-eight mark on the syringe she drew another two units and tapped the needle with a fingernail. Next step was to eliminate any air bubbles. Or was that just for intravenous injections? She'd seen this a hundred times on TV. As expected, a bubble of air floated to the top of the barrel. Eve withdrew the needle from the vial and pressed the plunger. A feeble squirt of liquid spilled into the air and ran down her index finger. The air bubble vanished leaving exactly twenty-eight units.

She found an alcohol swab in the bathroom cabinet and opened the aluminum foil. She looked at Brittany with a hopeful expression. "You ready?"

Brittany stroked the flesh just below her navel. "Here."

"Okay." She leaned forward and swabbed the skin with the pad. Without knowing how deep to insert the needle tip, she pushed it into her flesh, a quarter inch, then a little deeper until Brittany gasped with a shallow moan. Then she gently depressed the plunger and watched as the insulin slipped into her body.

"Okay, let's set you down on the bed for a while." She led her back to the bedroom, tugged the top cover into place, and helped Brittany settle in for a rest.

Brittany's eyes closed in a slow, drowsy faint as she drifted into a space that Eve would never know. She pulled the cover up to Brittany's shoulders and studied her face. What a time they'd had. With luck, it would soon be over. She gave her hand a light squeeze, then walked to the sliding glass door that led onto the tiny concrete patio. She stood a moment and looked into the shrubs and redwood trees.

That's where I'll wait, she decided and once again cinched the strap of the AR-15 over her shoulder. She drew the glass door along its track and took up a position in the woods where she could see anyone approach and still monitor Brittany's recovery through the glass door. She slumped down on her buttocks and leaned against the tree trunk. She peeled the wrapper from a granola bar, chewed off the end, and studied her surroundings. Then she opened the water bottle, took a long drink, and settled in to wait for the FBI.

Only one thing remained. To find Will while they were both still alive.

CHAPTER TWENTY-EIGHT

STANDING NEXT TO the window in the reception lobby, Dogboy watched Brittany drive the Hummer through the parking lot and coast down the east end toward Cottage Row. He ran a hand under his mask and scratched his beard. *Jasper. Where the hell is she going?*

He hated the itch of a three-day beard. Somehow the balaclava made the prickling on his face even worse. When he knew he was alone, he tugged off the mask and looped it under his belt. But never when Skipper was around mind you. No one wanted to risk the sharp bite of his bark.

He strolled down the hallway to the john where he and Finch had battled the fire. Gotta hand it to him, Finch was one tough customer. Fighting the smoke and flames without a mask the whole time. He'd met two troopers patrolling the Mexican border who could walk the roads and dirt trails barefoot. Two out of what? — two hundred plus. Finch could join their rank. Easy. The other hundred and ninety-nine were tenderfoots.

He swung open the door to the bathroom stall where the

fire had started — or according to Skipper – where Finch had lit the fuse. Maybe, maybe not. Either way, his wife had made a clean break and that seemed to worry Skipper more than anything else right now. More than the fact that Claws had disappeared. According to Jasper, Claws hadn't contacted her either. Not a word. Which, when you think about it, is very unusual. For old hatchet hand not to call his main squeeze — that spelled trouble.

Dogboy studied the charred hole in the toilet stall. To prove Finch had lit the fire, Skipper had hacked away at the breech from the kitchen and now it almost looked wide enough for someone to squeeze through into the galley. Why he did that was anybody's guess. That was just the Skipper. A force unto himself.

He squatted next to the toilet to take a closer look. Could someone jam through the gap? Maybe. He scooched onto his hands and knees and pressed his head into the opening. Then he wrapped an arm around the base of the toilet bowl and tried to wedge his body into the next room. Well, maybe not. The worst thing would be to get stuck and have to call for help. Leaving Skipper on his own to guard the scum.

He extracted himself from the gap and stood above the toilet bowl to relieve himself. He checked his watch. Coming up to 1600 hours. Time to spell off Skipper so he could contact the First Freedom Corps HQ. Tonight they were scheduled to stage their retreat at 0200. The plan was to wait til the prisoners drifted off, then make their way to the Hummer and drive off in the night. Like a fog lifting into the air. Not a sound. Not a breeze. Just disappear like ghosts.

He zipped up his fly and pressed the toilet handle. Nothing. He tried to flush again. "Hmmpf. Guess that's one more chore for the maintenance chief to fix." For a moment he pondered what it would be like to run a resort like Big River.

"Boring," he mumbled as he pulled the mask over his face. He adjusted the eye and mouth holes then made his way back to the dome where everyone was racked out on the floor. Next to the door, Skipper sat in a chair, his rifle cradled in the crook of his left arm.

"Everything under control?"

Skipper looked at him and let out a light snort as if the question were meaningless. "You?"

"Yeah." He waved a hand to the reception hall. "I just saw Jasper drive the Hummer through the parking lot."

"What?"

"Yeah." Dogboy sniffed the dome's stagnant air. Too many people sitting too long with nothing more to do than cough, sneeze, snore, and fart. "Just now."

Skipper shook his head with a look of disbelief. He stood up and wagged a finger toward the hallway. "Come here."

Dogboy followed then leaned against the door frame where he could keep an eye on the prisoners.

"So where'd she get off to anyways?" No sooner did he ask this question than he tried to swallow every word. Skipper's eyes widened with a scornful look, the sort of expression he put on when his temper was about to burst.

"I sent her to the Hummer to grab the zip ties." His wrist curled in the direction of the service yard.

"Oh yeah?" The question hung between two opposite poles.

Between Dogboy's need to know what Jasper was up to and his fear of asking Skipper a pointed question. Skipper, the bully of pain. Nonetheless, he pressed for more. "What'd we need the ties for?"

Skipper's eyes narrowed as if he was mulling over an answer that would satisfy this clown. He realized he needed to draw Dogboy under his wing the way he'd brought Jasper onside. "Change of tactics."

"What kinda change?"

"The job's done, Dogboy. I think we all know it. All we need to do is secure the scum" — he tipped his chin toward the Rotunda — "then check out."

"Like this afternoon?" An excitable edge rose in his voice. "Jeez, Skipper, I've been thinking the same thing all morning."

"Good. Then it's a done deal."

Skipper turned his head to one side, then back to consider Dogboy's lazy posture. Leaning on the door like that, his feet crossed with one ankle behind the other, his AR-15 propped against his thigh, his fingers toying restlessly with the bottom of his mask. All of it looked lazy — part of his hang-dog look.

"Tell me something." He leaned closer. "Where'd you get that name?"

"What name?"

"Dogboy. Who laid that on you?"

"Border patrol. Chasing wetbacks across the Tex-Mex line."

A dismissive chuckle sputtered out of Skipper's throat. "So you were what? Like a sheepdog chasing boys back across the Rio Grande?"

Dogboy's eyes narrowed to two tight slits. *Enough is enough.* Still, better to keep your gob shut. Especially when Skipper's mood has taken a positive swing. He shouldered his rifle and took a step toward the dome. "It's my watch," he muttered. "I'll — "

"No," Skipper interrupted. "Go find Jasper and haul her back here. Clock's tickin' and we're a man down. We need those zip ties ASAP."

Dogboy nodded and walked down the hall to the reception desk and out the lodge door. He stepped onto the porch and looked down the length of the parking lot. No sign of the Hummer. As he stepped onto the gravel lot, he tugged off the balaclava and began to wonder. A man down. That meant Claws was out of action. Skipper knew something had happened to a key man. But what? One thing was certain, the Skipper kept all the secrets to himself.

Quiet. That was the word purring through his mind as he made his way along the west end of the lodge to the chip path. Quiet never sounded so good, a thought that made him chuckle. But it was true. First, no more orders from Skipper. Second, no whining from the prisoners. If he had his way, he'd set up home somewhere here in the forest, maybe on the slope of Snow Mountain. A place where he could park his four-by-four at the end of a dirt road that led to nowhere. Where he could stock up supplies for a couple of months, then fish and trap for whatever else he needed. Plant a veggie patch. Buy a generator. Maybe hook up an internet connection or a sat-phone. A one-way phone so he could call out, but nobody could reach him. Then he'd be off the grid and live like every self-respecting soul he'd ever admired. Who are few and far between, he had to admit.

The exact opposite to all the prisoners they'd corralled in the dome. That was the one thing Skipper had right. "Before you drain the swamp," he'd said, "first you have to skim off the scum." Or the way Claws put it, "Scrub the scum."

The scum who made up all the fake news. Christ, what two-faced liars. Denying the election had been stolen! Along with the media stars and the Hollywood glam-boys, the gays, the fembots, and trannies. But we put 'em in their place. Damn right. Now they know the price they'll pay if they carry on down that road.

A hundred feet along the path he spotted the Hummer parked on one side of the trail. He scratched the back of his head.

"What the hell?"

He slid the AR-15 strap from his shoulder and stopped to survey the surrounding cottages. He scanned the nearby trees and shrubs. Nothing.

"Jasper?" His voice soft, just above the fading breeze ticking through the tree limbs above.

He gripped the rifle handguard in his left hand and slipped the fingers of his right along the trigger guard. He walked in a wide arc so he could examine the driver's side of the truck. Then he understood. Somehow Jasper lost control of the Hummer and crashed headlong into the concrete electrical box. He moved around to study the impact point, his eyes wide with disbelief. "Damn you, Skip," he muttered. Before they loaded the Hummer, he told Skipper to attach a bull bar to the front bumper so they could avoid this exact problem. But, oh no. Skipper had dismissed his advice with a sneer.

"Asshole," he mumbled as he touched the crushed hood of the Hummer with the palm of his hand. Still warm. A dirty gray vapor rose from somewhere inside the engine block.

He felt his heart jump as he considered the implications. Plan A, out the window. Which meant no way out tonight. Or not. Maybe they could take the resort service truck. Better still, borrow the rides from the scum. Why not? They had all the prisoners' car keys. In fact, it'd be smarter to take two or three vehicles to branch out and cover their getaway.

But where the hell did Jasper get off to?

He continued to walk along the trail, scanning each of the cabins as he prowled from one side of the path to the other. Then he noticed the door on the Redwood. Yesterday in his search for Brittany he'd tossed the cottage from top to bottom. Claws had already given it the once-over, but he decided to take a second look. On his way out, he'd closed the door. Snug tight. But now here it is, open just a crack.

He pulled the AR-15 strap over his left shoulder and drew his pistol into his right hand. He approached the cottage from the side, then slipped around to the sliding glass door on the back deck. He leaned forward to peer through the glass and cupped a hand over his eyes to block the reflective glare.

He pointed the Glock at the door and with two fingers of his left hand slid it open. When the bottom of the door squealed in the track he dashed into the room and locked his arms in a firing position. There she lay. Jasper lying on the bed, a sheet pulled up to her chin.

"Jasper?" His arms dropped to his waist and he stepped over to the foot of the bed. "Jasper? You okay?"

She stirred slightly as her eyes blinked open.

"What the?" In an instant it hit him. The fembot who'd run off on day one. He lifted the pistol and lined up a shot that would hit her square in the chest. "Who the fuck are you?"

Brittany pushed herself up onto an elbow. It took a moment for her to understand. A cammie. About to shoot her. "No. *Hey, no!*" She waved a hand as if she could block the bullets about to rip into her body.

Dogboy pivoted on the ball of his foot and did a quick sweep of the room. He stepped into the bathroom, pulled the shower curtain aside then walked back to confront Brittany.

"Where the hell is Jasper?" He leaned forward, his chest hovering above her.

"Who?" She sat up and ran a hand over her face. She could feel a dash of adrenaline jet through her chest and arms. Into her head. Where was Eve?

"Jasper!" He slapped her face with his open hand. "Wake the fuck up! Where's Jasper?"

"Oww. Stop," she whimpered and buried her face in both hands. She dragged in a lungful of air, her chest taut with fear. Would he hit her again? Her teeth ground together as she prepared for another blow.

"I said, where's Jasper?"

She glared at him. "You don't want to know."

"Oh yes I do, bitch."

She arched her back and let out a scream. "Eve!" Her voice filled the cottage. *"Eve! Help!"*

A look of contempt etched his face as he considered what to do. He could drag her back to the resort and let Skipper deal with her. But it would be best if he could find Jasper and return to the dome with both women in tow. All right, he told himself, just beat the answer out of her. Knowing that was the only way, he leaned forward again and slapped her twice more. The blows came fast and hard. A line of spittle drizzled from her mouth and she spat out a dash of blood.

"I'm right here, Honey."

Dogboy turned toward the sliding glass door and saw Eve with an AR-15 braced against her shoulder. Her forefinger slipped from the guard onto the trigger, ready to fire.

CHAPTER TWENTY-NINE

"EVE! HELP!"

Eve woke with a start. Brittany's scream shuddered through her body and Eve's arms flew up in a panic. The open bottle — perched in her lap while she dozed off — splashed a dash of water over her thighs and into the parched soil at the base of the redwood tree.

In one move she sprang to her feet and slipped the butt of the AR-15 against her shoulder. As she stole across the ground to the open glass door she saw Dogboy leaning over Brittany, his Glock pistol in his right hand. When he slapped Brittany's face, Eve crept into the cottage, took two steps toward the bed, and aimed her weapon at Dogboy's spine.

She set her feet, aligned her posture, and drew a breath. When her friend called again, she spoke up.

"I'm right here, Honey."

The sound of her own voice brought a grin to her lips. Honey? Hell, why not? Brittany was the closest she'd come to a real girlfriend since Gianna Whitelaw had been murdered.

Dogboy turned and a sorry look crossed his face. Without the balaclava mask, Eve could see his stark, handsome features. A straight nose, full lips, high cheekbones, and a wide lantern jaw with a dimple notched into his chin. He stood about five-ten or -eleven, his eyes were ice blue. If it weren't for his ridiculous name, more than a few women would try him on for size.

"You."

"Yeah. Me. I'm back." Her eyes narrowed as she held his gaze. She could see him calculating the odds. Does she have the guts to shoot me? What are my chances?

"Don't even think about it, Dogboy. Two hours ago I unloaded six rounds into Claws. If you want it bad enough, you can have your fair share, too."

"Claws?" His voice wavered with a hint of disbelief.

A moment of silence passed between them. Another. His pistol was still trained on Brittany, but when he turned to confront Eve, he'd lost a beat. He was one note off the current rhythm and he knew he couldn't recover. He was outgunned and outmaneuvered. His shoulder shrugged and he nodded at Eve with a look of defeat.

She smiled to acknowledge his choice. And she could see how it would all play out now. How she'd move all three of them from this moment to some inexact time ahead when she'd won another round. But only if she could find Will. Find him alive. That would take her to the endgame.

She tipped her head toward the bathroom. "Brit, get out of bed and stand next to the door."

Brittany roused herself and moved quickly toward the

bathroom door. She'd partially recovered from the insulin crash. Enough to follow Eve's directions.

"Dogboy, toss your Glock next to the bureau. And the knife. Then down on your knees."

"What the–"

"Do it or die!" Eve screamed and fired a rifle burst into the closet mirror. Three or four rounds lit up the air and the glass exploded into the spare bedding, pillows, and blankets stored on the upper shelf.

The blast was deafening. Brittany clasped her hands over her ears. Dogboy let out a cry of pain and tossed the pistol and knife toward her, then settled on his knees with a gasp of exasperation.

Eve turned her jaw to one side. The explosive gunshots caught her by surprise. Her basic weapons training had failed her. She shook her head with a look of regret but determined to carry on. "Brit, pass me the knife."

"My God, Eve. Don't do that again without warning me."

She handed the blade to Eve.

"Good. Now take the pistol and point it at the back of his head."

"His head?"

"Yeah. Just like before with Claws. Stand behind him. Remember what I said. Keep your finger next to the trigger. But don't hesitate to kill him if he makes a move."

"Hey, ladies, let's slow it down, okay?"

Brittany pressed her lips together, picked up the pistol, and took up her position as instructed. "Got it."

"Okay, Dogboy. We're slowing down. Just like you wanted.

Now lie on your belly and slip off the AR-15. Slow and steady. Got it?"

"Yeah, yeah," He lay on his stomach, then struggled to loosen the strap and wrench the rifle from his shoulder. When he managed to uncinch it, he slid the weapon across the floor toward Eve. "Now what?"

"On your hands and knees."

She swung the desk chair into the open space between the bed and the desk.

"Now crawl over to the chair here."

She knocked a leg of the chair with the toe of her shoe. When he'd made his way across the room, she waited for him to look up at her. Then she lifted the barrel of her AR-15. A motion to get him to sit up.

"Be a good doggie," she chided. "Into the chair. Up you go."

She backed three paces away from the chair. When he was sitting, she gestured to Brittany. Eve took a moment to consider how well her friend was holding up. Clearly, the medication had stabilized her mood and reflexes.

"Now stand behind him, Brit. Same deal. Gun at the back of his head. If he so much as farts — kill him."

"Got it."

Eve set both AR-15s against the wall, pulled the zip ties she'd taken from the Hummer, and snapped them tight between her hands. "All right, Dogboy. Hands on the armrests."

When he could see what was coming, he let out a groan. "Hey, com'on. We don't need to do this."

"No? I think we do." Eve fastened his wrists to the chair

arms, then strapped his ankles to the legs. When he was secured, she stood beside him and nodded at Brittany.

"Okay, now we can relax a minute. Brit, I want you to sneak along the bushes to my cabin." She tipped her head to the right. "The Sugar Pine, at the end of the trail. The door's probably still open. Get us some water from the refrigerator. And grab any leftover food. Then we can all sit and chat for a while."

As Brittany stepped through the sliding door onto the patio, Eve sat on the edge of the bed and studied her captive without saying a word. She wanted the silence to make him wilt. Five minutes later Brittany returned with three water bottles in her hands and a sandwich tucked under her arm. She gave two bottles and the sandwich to Eve.

"So. This is all very simple now," she said to Dogboy. "There's only one question you have to answer." She put on a stone face and waited until he blinked. "Answer it and you'll live."

His lips snarled with a look of loathing. "Don't kid yourself, Noon. If I don't get back to the lodge in the next five minutes, Skipper and Jasper will be down here with guns blazing."

"Hmm. 'Fraid not. We've got breaking news, Dogboy." She wondered how to phrase it. The answer was always the same: straight up. "Jasper and Claws are both dead. And half an hour ago, I spoke to the San Francisco Chief of Special Operations." She glanced at the ceiling. "A SWAT team chopper should be here any minute now."

He took a moment to think. He figured the business about a

chopper was a dodge. Something to throw him off balance. But Jasper? "What'da'ya mean? She's dead?"

She considered how much to reveal, and decided she held more power over him if she held something back. She uncapped two bottles, took a drink from one, and held the other beneath his chin. "Drink?"

"What happened to her?"

"You want some water or not?"

He nodded with a doleful look. She held the bottle to his lips and watched him slurp down a mouthful. She set the bottle aside and peeled the cellophane wrapper from the sandwich pack, tugged a triangle wedge into her fingers, and held it up to the light as if she had to examine it for flaws. She passed the other half of the sandwich to Brittany.

"You know, before we go any further, I need you to tell me where I can find Will Finch." She began to chew her sandwich with slow deliberation.

"First you tell me what happened to Jasper."

"Claws cracked her skull open with a steel pole." She shrugged with a sorrowful look. "There was nothing we could do. Bad karma, I guess. You know, with you guys terrorizing everyone for the last two days."

"Bullshit."

"It's true," Brittany said, walking past Eve and sitting on the second chair. She took a bite from her sandwich and paused to look up at the ceiling. In the distance, they could hear the sound of a helicopter hovering for a moment. Then the sound faded and the room fell into silence.

"So Dogboy, listen up. You hear that? That chopper's going

to put down an FBI SWAT team at the service yard. They should be here in" — she checked her watch — "ten minutes or so. Now if I haven't found my husband by then, I'm going to untie you, shoot you in the pecker, and wait five minutes while you think it over. After that, I'll put a round through your forehead. Then to make it look like self-defense, I'll fire a burst from your AR-15 into the woods. Your prints are already smeared all over the 15. No one will question what happened."

She pointed to the forest through the glass door and swallowed another drink of water.

"So it's your call." She took a deep breath, then screamed, *"WHERE'S MY HUSBAND?!"*

The sound of her voice sent a shiver through him. "Okay. All right! Jasper took him yesterday. If she's dead, how the hell am I supposed to know where he is?"

Brittany lifted Dogboy's pistol in her free hand and stared at him. "That's not good enough," she whispered.

He studied her face for a moment then turned to Eve. "What's wrong with her?"

"Insulin crash," Brittany replied in a serious tone. "Makes me a little jittery." She lifted the Glock, took what appeared to be a haphazard aim, and fired a shot above Dogboy's head. The loud burst served to amplify her rage. *"Now where the hell is Will Finch?"* she screamed.

"What the fuck?" He let out a whimper as he ducked his chin onto his chest. A line of sweat burst across his forehead. "Wait, wait, wait."

"Look, asshole," Brittany continued, "I've been starved, chased into the woods by that hand-job friend of yours, deprived of food, water, medicine, sleep — *and now I'm ready to fucking kill someone.* Tell us where Finch is, or you are done!"

"All right! Okay." He glanced at Eve. "Skipper told me she took him out behind the A-frame. Somewhere behind the lodge," he added. He decided to omit the fact that Jasper had killed him. He'd heard the kill shots. Two of them. Everybody had. But better not to let on.

Eve nodded. The expression on her face revealed a mix of emotions. Hope, fear, dread. "The A-frame?"

"Yeah. Where the maintenance guy lives."

The sound of the helicopter whirled above them again. Then faded once more.

"He better be there, Dogboy. If not, I'll be back for you." Eve grabbed his AR-15 by the handguard and quickly released the magazine, checked its capacity, and shoved it into her front pocket. She tucked the Sig26 under her belt beside the knife. She had a rifle, a pistol, and a knife. She clenched her teeth together and whispered to herself. *Ready.*

She grabbed her water bottle and wrapped an arm around Brittany's shoulders. "Okay. You have the only loaded weapon. Understand?"

"Yeah."

"Don't let him loose."

"Okay. But can I kill him?"

A look passed between them. A silent understanding.

Eve winked at her. "Sure. If you feel the urge."

CHAPTER THIRTY

EVE CLOSED THE front door to the Redwood cottage and took a moment to examine the surrounding cabins and the forest that stood behind them. She could feel her heart thrumming in her chest. Her head swept from side to side, scanning the woods for Skipper or the SWAT team. The weight of the struggles with Claws, Jasper, and Dogboy pressed down on her shoulders and she took a moment to try to clear her mind. For the first time in two days, she had a moment to reflect on her own. She could see the kaleidoscope of events flash in front of her eyes.

The moment when Claws hammered Jasper. The look on her face as she fell to the ground. The volcanic rage erupting from him when he realized what he'd done. Then his blind charge at Eve, the soft jolt of her weapon as it fired round after round at his head. Boom, boom, boom. How many rounds did it take to kill him? Take *you* to kill him. She brushed a hand over her eyes when reality hit. You killed a man. *Again*. She slumped onto the front porch of the cottage and felt the tears flowing from her eyes.

Get past it, she told herself. That's done. Now move forward. And where in hell is the SWAT team? She gazed at the heavy clouds packing together above the forest. They'd heard the chopper hover above them, then fade away. Twice they'd heard it. Dogboy and Brit, both of them looked stunned when they realized the game could soon be over.

Okay, but so what? Until you see the FBI in the flesh, you're still on your own. Find Will. That's all you've got to do now. *Find him. Find him and hold onto him like life itself.* She braced the handguard of AR-15 in the crook of her left elbow, stood up, and stepped from the porch onto the trail.

As she walked up the path toward the lodge, the depth of her crisis continued to hit her. She felt it — a gut punch radiating through her belly and across her chest. *"What the fu—?"* she gasped and swung around looking for a new attacker. No one. Then she sensed her knees wobbling. Just ahead stood the wrecked Hummer. She lurched forward and braced her hands on the crumpled hood.

"Omigod," she whimpered as she struggled to breathe. "No. No, not now."

Her knees collapsed under her and her arms slid along the Hummer's front tire as she slumped onto the ground. She tried to bottle up the panic and concentrate on the feeling in her lungs. On simply breathing. *In, out, hold.* She'd experienced a panic attack twice during her time with the SFPD. But never like this. She released the AR-15, wrapped both arms around her chest, and pulled her knees up to her belly. She managed to draw a few shallow breaths then realized that lying in the dirt in a fetal position blocked her from filling her lungs with air.

With oxygen. She could almost taste it flushing across her tongue. She managed to unfurl her legs and arms. In, out, hold. Repeat. In, out, hold.

How long did it take to recover? Ten, fifteen minutes? She lifted her hand and glanced at her watch. 4:47. You have an hour, maybe two before dusk. Two hours to find Will but here you are, lying on your f-ing butt. Get up, woman. "Come on, get up!" she mumbled.

"Ma'am?"

The voice startled her. Her head twisted around. "What?"

"Ma'am, are you all right?"

She wiped the back of her wrist over her eyes. "Hunh?"

"Can you sit up, Ma'am?"

She blinked. He wore a black para-military outfit. The word SWAT was emblazoned on his jacket in bold white caps. He wore a steel helmet. Kevlar armor and pads were strapped over his jacket and pants. His elbow and knee pads seemed to bud from his arms and legs.

Suddenly a shocked look crossed his face. "Ma'am, back away from your weapons." The compassion in his voice dissolved. "The rifle and the handgun."

"What?"

He aimed a pistol at her chest. "Ma'am, move away from your weapons and give me your hand." He didn't wait for her to comply. In two quick moves he pulled her Sig26, the AR-15 magazine, and the knife from her belt. He lightly frisked her then grabbed her by the wrist and dragged her along the side of the Hummer where he released her next to the shrubs.

"What are you doing with all these weapons?"

"I'm sorry," she offered, clearing her throat. Yes, you can breathe now, she assured herself. "It's not *my* rifle." She tried to make it sound like an apology. "Or the pistol."

"Ma'am, what's your name?"

"Eve," she coughed. "Eve Noon."

"Noon." His eyes swept across her face as if he needed to assure himself of something. "I'm Sergeant Jake Connor. Did you call this in?"

"Yeah. Yes, I did." It came to her as a fraught memory. Then everything tumbled out at once. "I called Chief Wainwright" — now the details began to fall into place — "Victor Wainwright, the Chief of Special Operations at SFPD. Look, you've got to get up to the lodge. There's over thirty hostages. In the Rotunda. Skipper, he's the leader — you have to stop him. He's armed... Look, he's crazy — he'll kill them all unless — "

Connor held up a hand to silence her. Then he unclipped a com device from his vest and tapped a button. A soft squelch sputtered from the phone.

"Macron here. What d'you got Connor?"

"I've got her, sir. Eve Noon."

"Noon? How is she?"

Connor studied her face again. "I think she's recovering from shock. No apparent injuries." He put the mic aside and asked her, "Any injuries, Ms. Noon?"

"None stopping me." She lifted both hands in a gesture of surrender. "But my friend is diabetic. She's having a diabetic crash. Do you have any insulin supplies?

"No, she's good, sir," he added. "But someone here is in a

diabetic crash. Can you send a runner down with some insulin?"

During a lull, Eve could hear some background chatter on the other end of the mic.

"Okay. We can do that. Meanwhile, what's the sitrep?"

"I'm two hundred yards down the line of cabins east of the lodge. I'm stationed next to a damaged Hummer. It's out of commission. I think that means the terrorists have no wheels."

"That could make them more dangerous."

A pause. Eve heard Macron relay the message to some squad members.

"Any sign of the hostages?"

"Noon says there's thirty or more in the lodge Rotunda. The top dog, a dude named Skipper, is threatening them with weapons."

"What's the arsenal?"

Conner looked at Eve. "Do you know what kind of weapons they have?"

"AR-15s, pistols, knives."

He repeated the inventory to his commander.

"Okay, Connor. Hold your position. I'll be down there in five."

"Copy that, sir."

Their clockwork movement was exact. Minutes later, Lieutenant Macron arrived with two others, all of them equipped with similar weapons and tactical gear. To Eve the men looked almost identical. While she could make out the unique lines of their individual faces under their helmets, they all bore the same glum expression as they hunched beside her and Connor.

"Ms. Noon, I'm Lieutenant Gerold Macron." He pointed to the men beside him. "This is Charelli and Hindman. I understand you called this in."

She brushed some tears from her eyes, then said, "I did. That was me."

"Are you aware of what transpired a mile east of here?" When she didn't respond, he sensed he needed to add a human touch. He slipped off his helmet. "Back in the service yard" — he crooked a thumb along the path — "There's a tarp. A tarp covering — "

"Covering two bodies," she interrupted. "Claws and Jasper. He killed her. The man, I mean. He killed the woman. Then, uh … then when he tried to kill Brittany and me, I had to shoot him." She shrugged and twisted the cap off her water bottle. Then she twisted it back on, then off again. Finally, she took a shallow drink.

"We know you did, Ma'am."

She let out a light gasp and studied his face. How could he know that? She took another drink and decided it didn't matter.

"But that's not on you." He touched her shoulder with his hand, his fingers soft there, almost tender. "You did the right thing. It's exactly what I would've done. No one here would do any different. Do you understand?"

"Yes."

"Good." He nodded as if they'd reached an accord. But now he had to press on. "Ms. Noon, who's Brittany?"

"My friend. She's diabetic and lost her insulin." She swept a line of perspiration from her forehead. "She's been crashing all afternoon. Do you have any insulin?"

He nodded. "Brought it with me."

She let out a long sigh of relief. Finally.

"So who is she?"

"She's the only one they didn't get. I mean I had to escape, but they *never* got her." She glanced at her cottage. The front door was still closed. "She's babysitting Dogboy."

"Dogboy?" A perplexed look crossed his face.

"The third terrorist. He's zap-strapped in a chair." She smiled. Zip-tied, zap-strapped? Who cared what you call it? For the first time, the absurdity of it all triggered a short rattle of laughter that erupted from her chest. "Sorry," she apologized, but a contrite chuckle undercut her regret. The laughter appeared to re-energize her.

"A third terrorist?" He studied her face. Her giggling suggested some kind of mental instability. Was she suffering the first symptoms of PTSD? He'd seen dozens of men and women hit the wall in similar circumstances. "Look, we have to lock him down right now."

"No." Now her voice hardened. Eve felt her stomach fluttering again. "They've taken my husband somewhere else. First, you help me find him, then I'll take you to Dogboy."

He nodded with an almost imperceptible shift of his head. "Your husband. What's his name?"

"Will Finch."

"Do you know where they've taken him?"

"Somewhere behind the A-frame." She felt a brief tinge of optimism. Macron was asking all the right questions. Maybe he'd lead her to him right now. "The A-frame's behind the lodge," she added. "Maybe a hundred feet behind the kitchen."

"All right. Good." He smiled. "I'll assign one of my men to it. But my orders are to follow an operational plan. First, contain the lodge and everyone within it. Which is in play as we speak. I'm sure you understand that saving the most lives possible is our first order of command."

She nodded.

"So right now, I have to secure this other man, Dogboy."

"No. Before I move another step. You have to find my husband."

Macron let out an exasperated sigh. Then he pulled a radio mic from his belt and clicked a switch. "Suzuki, have you secured the lodge perimeter?

After a pause, Suzuki replied. "Five more minutes, sir."

"Who's assigned to the kitchen wing?"

"That'd be Van Heusen and Scanlan."

"Copy that. Advise Van Heusen that one of the hostages has been taken somewhere behind the A-frame. Will Finch. When he has the liberty to perform a search — *and only then* — order Scanlan to flush out Finch and bring him to me at the command post.

"Copy, that sir."

Macron put the mic away and turned to Eve. "Ms. Noon, that's the best I can do. Now please take me to the third man."

Eve understood that any more negotiations would be fruitless. Finding Will had dropped to the bottom of Macron's to-do list. What were her options? None. She inhaled a deep breath, stood up, and took a moment to find her balance. "All right. I'll take you to them."

Lieutenant Macron ordered Connor and Charelli to stand

watch at the Hummer, waved a hand to Hindman, and said, "With me."

Then he matched his pace to Eve's weary gait as she led the way along the trail back to the Redwood Cabin.

CHAPTER THIRTY-ONE

AS EVE PEERED through the glass door into the Redwood, she could see Dogboy still strapped to the chair. His fingers clung to the ends of the chair arms in a classic white-knuckle grip. His hair was ruffled and mussed. Had Brittany been tussling his head? Whatever had transpired, Dogboy did not appear too pleased. Brittany sat on the edge of the bed, her pistol braced in her right hand as if she was about to fire a round into Dogboy's crotch. Eve didn't know whether she should laugh or gasp in surprise when she saw Brittany tugging at Dogboy's earlobe with her free hand. There was something sexual in the gesture. Kinky. After a moment she decided to bottle up her reaction and let Macron deal with the situation.

"Please. *Please,* put that away," Dogboy begged. "Or point it somewhere else!"

"Okay. How 'bout your left ear?" Her voice lilted with a soft tease as if she couldn't be happier. "Or maybe the tip of your nose?"

Macron stepped through the glass doorway with his rifle

poised to shoot her in the chest. Hindman stepped behind him, followed by Eve.

"Ma'am, drop your weapon now!" Macron barked. "I will not hesitate to shoot you!"

Brittany's face blanched as her pistol dropped to the floor. "Omigod," she whimpered. "I'm sorry. I'm *so* sorry." She leaned toward Dogboy and for a moment it looked like she might embrace him.

"Get her the fuck away from me," Dogboy squealed. "She's one crazy bitch!"

Hindman grabbed her weapon and tucked the pistol into the back of his belt. Macron shook his head and relaxed his posture. Everyone drew a breath and an air of relief flushed through the room.

One more potential disaster averted, Eve thought and then took her friend into her arms. "It's over now, Brit. Really. It's all done. You can go home to your son. We both can."

Macron took a moment to search the room and bathroom. Satisfied that the women could pose no threat, he instructed Hindman to unstrap Dogboy from the chair, cuff him and lift him to his feet. He then radioed a situation report to their command post. With the procedural requirements in hand, he stood face-to-face with his captive.

"What's your name, son?"

Son? Macron had ten, maybe fifteen, years on Dogboy. Nonetheless, Eve could barely believe her ears, then she realized that Macron was launching another ploy. A master of mind games, he could quickly set the tone to win any matchup in his own way. He'd done it with her. She'd refused to lead him to Dogboy before he found Will. Now here she stood watching Macron unspool his new quarry.

Dogboy refused to look him in the eye.

"Son, the jig is up. Two of your squad are dead. The ones you call Claws and Jasper. They're lying under a tarp at the service yard."

A miserable look crossed his face and he glanced at Eve.

"Like we told you," Eve said as if she was offering condolences. "They're gone."

"And Skipper's holed up in the lodge alone. I have him surrounded by fifteen SWAT veterans." He paused to let the implications sink in. "Believe me when I say this, we don't make mistakes. Not one in ten years."

" — " Dogboy gasped something incoherent.

"So let's start with your name, son."

A pause. "Daniel," he whispered.

"Daniel?"

"Daniel Smith," he said in a more steady voice. A voice reconciled to complete defeat.

"Nice to meet you, Daniel. I'm Lieutenant Gerold Macron. This is Vince Hindman." He tipped his chin to Hindman. "The three of us are going to take a walk to the muster station we've set up. Got some coffee and sandwiches there. That sound good, Daniel?"

He shrugged and let out a moan. Macron nodded to Hindman who then led Dogboy by the elbow towards the door. Hindman stopped to wait for further orders.

Macron turned to Brittany, tipped his chin to one side, and smiled. "So I understand you need some insulin."

"Yes." Her eyes widened. "I have one vial left, but I'll need more soon."

He opened a patch pocket and pulled a sealed pouch into his hand. "I'm told this may cover you for a few days."

Brittany opened the pouch and glanced inside. She inhaled a long breath and closed her eyes. "Thank you." She gazed at him as if he might be an angel. "Thank you *so* much."

"You're welcome, ma'am." He glanced at Hindman. Hindman shifted his weight from foot to foot with an uneasy impatience.

"I'm sorry, ladies, but this isn't over yet. Soon, but not yet. I'm going to send someone down here to debrief you."

Eve and Brittany traded a look. "Fine," Eve dug her hands into her pockets. "Whatever it takes," she said, burying her desperation to find Will.

"If you need anything," Macron said as he left the cabin, "ask Sergeant Connor and Charelli up near the Hummer."

The two women stood at the open door as the three men marched up the path. Then Eve looked over to Brittany.

"You okay? I mean with the insulin." She rolled her lips together, wondering if she should ask Brittany to help her.

"Yeah. Mostly." She swiveled her head in the direction of the path where the men turned to the left and walked out of view. "They seem like gods to me," she said and dismissed an urge to chant another Hail Mary.

They were alone now and Brittany felt a mix of emotions. Joy, gratitude, lingering anxiety about Will Finch. Embarrassment about Dogboy. Better to confess that to Eve, she thought. "I was just toying with Dogboy, you know. I was never going to fucking shoot him."

"I know. Of course." Eve chuckled, still amazed by how Brittany had wound him up.

"So look, Brit. I've got to find Will. But this whole thing is over for you now. Totally over." She embraced her in a light hug, then pulled away, her hands still set on Britanny's shoulders. "But can you help me find him?"

An uncertain pause welled between them. Britany wiped a smudge from her eyes and brushed a hand under her nose. It was as if she had to prepare herself.

"Eve, you saved my life. You know that, right?" Brittany pulled Eve back into a hug. "So don't even ask, okay? Let's go find him."

Chapter Thirty-Two

As Eve led Brittany toward the Sugar Pine cottage she couldn't stop thinking of Will. The night with him in bed, lying in his strong, thick arms as she opened herself to him. They really had something together. She and Will and their daughter Casey. Then it all crashed to a halt with the catastrophe brought on by Skipper, Jasper, Claws, and Dogboy. And now everything that followed Friday night led to this moment. Standing here in the forest, wondering where to find her husband.

"Brit, let's stop in the Sugar Pine. Is there any food left inside?

"Another sandwich, some water, and a chocolate bar."

"Good. Just in case we need it." Eve smiled at her. She appeared to be completely in control of herself. She'd avoided the insulin crash, or at least the worst part of it, and embraced the search for Will without any reservation.

Eve found two water bottles in the mini-refrigerator, a ham sandwich, and a Toblerone bar. Eve offered the chocolate to Brittany.

"You want it?"

She shook her head. "No, not with the insulin. It's like poison."

"Right. Of course," she said and gave a water bottle to Brittany and shoved the other supplies in her daypack. "Ready?"

"Yeah. The sooner the better." The lilt in her voice sounded optimistic, almost eager.

As usual, Eve led the way. She guided them to the end of the cottage trail and then pushed through the knee-high salal into the forest. When they passed three or four redwood trees, Eve pointed to a track on the left.

"Looks like another deer trail. We're going to have to swing left behind the lodge property, then find our way back in toward the A-frame."

"Where Dogboy said we'd find him."

"Yeah." She paused to listen to the helicopter sweeping above them somewhere to the south. "The main thing is to loop behind Macron's team. If they spot us, they'll lock us up."

"In the hoosegow."

Eve responded with an amused look. She hadn't heard the term in decades.

"That's what Jonny always says. Put the cammies in the hoosegow." She wrapped her arms together as if she was hugging him. "I miss the sound of his voice. You know, the crazy little things he says."

Eve ignored her mood change. "There's one cammie left, Brit. *Skipper.* And he's a total bastard." She held up a finger and added in a serious tone, "So look, silent running 'til we find Will, okay."

She nodded and they pressed on.

The deer track was narrow, maybe eight inches wide, but it cut a shallow rut into the forest floor. The air was cooled by a breeze that lifted the highest tree limbs into the slate-gray sky. They could see a mass of heavy clouds unfurl over the forest as the wind blew in from the Pacific. Eve could smell the threat of rain in the air. An aroma she could almost taste. As they walked on, they noticed two rectangular signs nailed to a post beside the trail. The top sign read: "Lodge Boundary." The second sign, fashioned in the shape of a hand with an index finger pointing to the north, read: "Pudding Creek — two miles." The deer trail continued in the direction of the creek.

"Let's go on another twenty yards or so," Eve whispered and pointed toward the creek. "Then cut around to the left. My guess is that should swing us back toward the lodge."

Brittany uncapped her water bottle and took a sip. "How far do you think?"

"Less than ten minutes." Eve didn't want to admit that they were more lost than found right now. But she had a decent sense of direction. And she'd been bolstered over the last two days hiking through the forest with nothing to guide her but the sun, a pocket compass, and dead reckoning. She took a long drink of water and glanced at Brittany. "Ready?"

Brittany bowed and waved a hand as if she was an usher opening a door to a mystery tour. "Lead on, woman. You haven't made a false step yet."

They crept through the forest, careful to lift their feet over tree roots and deadfall. When either of them snapped a twig underfoot, she would turn to the other with a guilty look. A nod and a smile provided forgiveness and they pressed on until Eve raised a hand. Brittany froze, then Eve beckoned her closer and whispered in Brittany's ear.

"See it?" Her hand pointed to a break between two birch trees. "Just to the left."

Brittany cleared a strand of hair from her face and stared at the top of the Rotunda roof. The clouds streaming above them cast a gray pallor over the dome.

"So that means the A-frame is somewhere over there?" She pointed to a stand of trees on Eve's right.

"I think so."

They both sipped another drink of water as they paused to consider what they might find. Now that they were this close, a feeling of dread welled through them. If Will was wounded — or worse — Eve didn't know how she'd react.

Brittany studied Eve's face. "You okay?"

She blinked and ignored the question. "Not a sound now."

Eve turned and led them in a direction that curled behind the back of the lodge. Maybe it was a hundred feet through the woods, maybe two. She felt as if she was wandering in a foggy maze. The effort to determine distance and direction became little more than a guessing game. Above all, she had to avoid Macron's men, who she knew would be stationed in a ring around the resort. Soon they came to a narrow clearing. A few raindrops flecked against her hands. She turned her face to the sky. Brittany stood beside her. They both ran their tongues over their lips as the light rain dotted their faces.

"Jeez, Eve. He could be anywhere around here," Brittany

said, "Maybe we should split up."

"I don't know. Dogboy said Jasper took him behind the A-frame." But where? A sense of ambivalence washed through her. Choosing any one direction seemed absurd. Go left, he might be lying in the dirt on her right. Go east, he could be west. North, south.

"Look, you go that way." Brittany pointed toward the lodge kitchen in the distance. She could make out the row of windows looking onto the weedy lawn and the steel exit doors that led from the kitchen to the A-frame. "I'll look for him over there, all right?" Her arm swung toward the Rotunda dome.

A puzzled look crossed Eve's face. Where was he? Why didn't he just stand up and call her?

"Okay, Eve?"

Okay, she told herself. Brit's right. Split up and double your chances of finding him. "Yeah. Like you said, head toward the dome. I'll go this way."

Eve stepped forward, crouching as she climbed over the tree roots, salal, and weeds surrounding the tall trees. Forty feet to her right stood a stand of three or four pine saplings nestled together. As she walked toward them she saw a ripple purl through their branches. She stopped and stared at the slight movement. Was it the wind? She crept forward. No. Then what?

CHAPTER THIRTY-THREE

As Skipper peered through a hexagonal window of the dome he brushed away a spider clinging to the glass and stomped it under his foot. Damn thing. He turned back to the window and frowned at the limited view. The outlook wasn't even close to the broad perspective he'd had from the lodge porch. It'd be better to stand in the reception room to assess his situation, but he didn't want to leave the scum unguarded. *The scum?* More like thirty shriveling worms. All of them stank now, but over the last night Kobayashi and his wife began coughing — a honking walrus bark — that kept everyone awake. Then there were the women. Two of them had to visit the women's toilet every few hours to tend to their business. You'd think God, back in the Garden of Eden, might've been kinder to the girl. But that's how he punished her — and all women forever after. Their crime? Deceiving their men.

He sucked his bottom lip between his teeth and considered his situation. Which is bad and getting worse, he decided. Claws gone AWOL. And now Jasper and Dogboy, the piece of crap, disappear along with the Hummer. Gone for an hour. Worst of all, the chopper hovering above the lodge, taking the measure of the place. Won't be long until some black shirts appear at the door demanding your surrender. Surrender! How the hell had it all gone so wrong so fast?

Skipper turned on his heel and swept his rifle above the heads of the enemy hunched on the floor. What a filthy bunch. It would be so easy to end them all right now. To unload a clip on those closest to the lobby door, reload and knock off the rest. *Surrender?* Think again a-hole.

"Skipper Jarvis."

When he heard the voice call his name, his reverie crashed to a halt. How did they know his name? He gripped his weapon in both hands, swung around, and stood poised to fire.

"Skipper Jarvis, my name is Lieutenant Gerold Macron. My SWAT team has surrounded the lodge." Macron paused so Skipper could absorb the full impact of his plight. "Claws and Jasper are dead. And Daniel Smith — Dogboy — is in custody."

Dogboy. Dogboy told them his name. And likely everything else.

"Skipper, your only chance to survive is to put down your weapons and come through the front door of the lodge with your hands up. Do you understand me?"

He smiled at that. A second-rate cliché from some second-rate cop. He shook his head at the thought of a B-movie actor playing his role on TV six months down the road. Well, this show doesn't end in defeat, he assured himself. Not yet.

He scanned the faces of his enemies cowering on the floor

of the dome. "One move from any of you and I will waste you all!" he screamed. He blasted a round of bullets into the ceiling. Seconds later three deflated balloons fluttered in a lazy dance to the floor.

A horrible moan rolled through the room. Half the men and women broke into sobs and clung to one another. As they froze in place, he made his way through the door into the lobby and took up a position next to the stained glass window overlooking the parking lot.

He attuned his ears to the words buzzing through a megaphone outside.

"Skipper, each building exit is covered by two men. I have a chopper flying surveillance. A fire and ambulance brigade are on the way from Mendocino."

He glanced at the vaulted ceiling. The chuk-chuk-chuk of helicopter blades clipped through the air. In the distance, he could make out the wail of sirens as they approached the lodge along the winding road through the forest.

"You don't have much time, Skipper."

"No. And neither do you," he whispered as if he needed to brace himself for what lay ahead.

He shifted his position to the left side of the door. The stained-glass window, a marvelous piece of art depicting the Big River Resort buried under a fresh winter snowfall, had one clear glass pane — a full moon gleaming its pure light on the world. Through the clear glass Skipper could survey the forces arrayed against him. Opposite the lodge door, about thirty yards away, on the far side of the gravel lot, five SWATers were deployed behind a row of parked cars. They wore black storm jackets, pants, Kevlar pads, and steel helmets. He guessed they were carrying the best equipment money could buy.

"And then some," he added as he weighed his options. "Best to take out the kingpin first. Next hit one or two others. Then make a dash-and-run."

He was starting to believe his luck was about to run hot. "Just like the old days with Hammer and Butch." His buddies from Task Force Destiny in Afghanistan. Back in '21 just before both of them died in a Taliban ambush. Just two months before the president — the lying thief — pulled the pin on the biggest military defeat since Vietnam.

He studied the SWATers as he waited for another prod from the megaphone. And then he saw the handheld bullhorn appear from behind a red Honda CRV.

"Skipper, listen up. Homeland Security just informed me that more troops will land here in thirty minutes. For your sake, I want to settle this before the cavalry arrives."

"The cavalry," he muttered with a sneer. He took a moment to line up a shot through the window. He knew that if he pressed the rifle muzzle against the clear window pane, the glass would barely distort the bullets' trajectory.

"Unleash a full clip at the bastard," he whispered.

Macron took a step forward and pressed his lips to the megaphone. "Skipper, time is running — "

Skipper fired, counting to five as the weapon blasted a dozen bullets into Macron's body. When the AR-15 discharged the last round, Skipper could hear the air resonate with the echoes of destruction. A collective gasp seemed to roll through the forest.

"Now move!" he screamed to himself as he dropped onto the floor and sprawled behind the reception desk. Seconds later a volley of bullets shattered the front door.

"Wakey-wakey, Macron. Or maybe you're just too dead." A smile twisted his lips as he inserted a new magazine into his rifle. He tipped his hand in mock gratitude to the SWAT leader. What a rookie move. Total amateur hour.

Chapter Thirty-Four

THE SOUND OF the helicopter sweeping above the lodge roused Finch from his sleepless nightmare. In an effort to lift his head, his face rubbed against the base of the tree trunk. He managed to move an inch or two, enough to feel the bark abrade the duct tape on his cheek. He gasped for air through his nostrils — and choked down another curse.

Shortly after Jasper had abandoned him he managed to keep his breathing under control. He'd forced himself to breathe in a steady cadence. Inhale for a count of five, hold for a count of five, exhale for five. A yoga technique he'd picked up from his first wife, Cecily.

The memory drew him into a long reverie. How they'd loved one another. Soon after they married, their son Buddy came along. Their familial bliss lasted three years. Until the day Cecily died of cancer. Within another two years, Finch lost Buddy, too. The alcoholic witch, Bethany — Finch's erstwhile girlfriend — had driven Finch's car into a concrete abutment. Buddy had been "riding shotgun," as he liked to say in his little sing-song voice. If only Bethany had buckled him into the backseat. That's all she'd had to do. She'd survived, but according to the medical examiner, Buddy died instantly. Because of the sharp blow to his head, he'd suffered no lingering pain. It was the one blessing Finch took to heart in the months following the loss of the boy and his mother.

Through the past night, as he lay strapped to the ground, Finch felt closer to them than he had in years. He'd never forgotten them, but with the passage of time, he'd found a new life with Eve and their daughter, Casey. And as he struggled to wrench his wrists free from the zip tie, his two wives and two children merged into one. They embodied a single sense of his life. A single purpose. Live for them, he whispered to himself. Both dead and alive, they are the center of your existence.

The sound of the helicopter meant something had changed. The terrorists' plan had faltered. In what way, he had no idea. But he understood that the chances of Jasper returning to free him were dashed. He was on his own. Images of trapped animals filled his mind. He'd heard enough hunters' tales of wolves and raccoons chewing off their limbs to free themselves of leg-hold traps. The price they paid to live another day.

Once again he turned his wrists inside the plastic strap using the trick he'd learned from the carjacker. When Jasper cinched him to the tree, Finch had butted his thumbs together to maximize the circumference around his hands. But Jasper's empty promise to free him, his exhaustion and hunger — all of it sent him into a cascading spiral. He knew this was his last chance. He either freed himself now or died here on his own.

Through the night he'd tried over and over to wrench his

hands free. Time to try again. He drew his elbows toward his shoulders and gained a small measure of mobility. Maybe two inches. But when he twisted his wrists together the plastic tore welts into his flesh. During the constant struggle over the past ten or twelve hours — he had no idea how long — he'd scored grooves into his hands that oozed trickles of blood along his forearms.

Now it dawned on him that he might have it all backward. Rather than drawing his elbows toward his head, he should extend them so that his hands stretched as far beyond the tree trunk as possible. That way the tension from the plastic tie might slack off. It was the lesson he'd learned as a boy when he played with a Chinese finger trap. Struggle and you are bound ever more securely. Relax and the bamboo trap slides away with little effort.

With his arms outstretched, he moved his wrists so that his palms drew together as if he had settled down to pray. Finger to finger, thumb to thumb. He eased one hand along the palm of the other and felt his fingers slipping apart. A quarter-inch. Another. Then his left hand slid under the plastic loop and it was free. Could it be that easy? He drew a deep breath, pulled both arms around the tree, turned on his hip, and sat up. He shook off the plastic zip tie from his right hand. Open wounds scored his flesh where the straps had gnawed at his wrists. A shiver of pain ran up his arms as he ran his fingers over the lacerations. Don't touch, he warned himself. Could become infected.

His right hand rose to his face and ran across the band of tape sealing his mouth. He let out a muffled gasp and drew a deep breath through his nostrils. A moment of panic seized him. He lurched forward. Breathe, he whispered to himself and once again he gained control through the cycle of yogic breathing.

When his sense of composure returned, he wedged a thumbnail under the tape below his left ear and peeled a corner free. He had at least three days of beard stubble stuck under the tape. One move, he thought. Then he tore the duct tape away in a single, fierce tug that peeled the band from cheek to cheek. As he cried out, Finch rolled onto the ground, his hands clutching his face as if the skin had been peeled from his jaw. His fingers ran back and forth over his cheeks, soothing the sting left by the harsh tear from the duct tape. When the pain subsided he sat up and examined the sticky side of the tape. Twenty or thirty whisker hairs clung to the band. But no sign of blood.

He let out a long gasp and shook his head from side to side, almost unable to believe that he'd survived. When he found his bearings he looked up to the sky and felt a few dots of rain sprinkling onto his face. He massaged the raindrops into his skin as if they might be a restorative gel.

The surrounding trees looked withered, barely alive. The drought had curled the pale green leaves into thin swatches resembling cardboard scraps. The dusty ground had been swept by the occasional windstorm which had loosened the topsoil. He examined a few stones nosing up through the soil and pulled a pointed rock into his left hand. Maybe the stones could cut through the plastic tie binding his legs together.

This might work, he thought and clawed through the dirt

until he upended a flat rock the size of a dollar pancake. He leaned forward and wedged the flat rock between his pant cuffs and the zip tie. Fortunately, Jasper had cinched his feet together, not at the ankles, but around the bottom of his jeans. "Thank you, Jasper," he whispered as he adjusted the flat rock so that it could serve as a striking plate.

Then he clutched the rock with the pointed tip in his fist and hammered the plastic tie against the strike plate. The reverberation sent a shock into his shins.

"Damn it!" He shook his head and cursed his stupidity. Then he unbuttoned his shirt, folded it over onto itself, flattened it into a narrow pad, and wedged it between the flat rock and his jeans. The zip tie was so tight that it took two or three minutes to fit the padding in place.

He drew another breath and struck the plastic with the pointed rock. The first strike felt hard against his leg, but he knew he could endure the dull pain. The padding did its job and he continued a steady hammering at the plastic tie.

Clack. Clack. Clack. He counted twenty-seven blows. On the twenty-eighth strike, the plastic split apart and fell onto the dead leaves that littered the ground. He was free.

One at a time, he lifted his ankles on his knees to examine the cuts and bloody scabs on the soles of his feet. The punishment he'd absorbed as he stumbled ahead of Jasper across the gravel path from the kitchen, past the A-frame, and into the forest. He knew they would take a while to heal.

He pushed himself onto his knees and scanned the surroundings. Behind him, the forest. On his left was the Rotunda and the door through which Eve had escaped. Ahead stood the

A-frame, the food locker, and the resort kitchen. He remembered when Jasper marched him into the forest he'd seen the food storage shed. And the padlock gaping open in the lock hasp.

Above all, he needed water now. He imagined he could find a stockpile of plastic water bottles stacked somewhere inside the shed. He took a half-step forward and winced at the pain in his feet. Nonetheless, he pressed on. Soon he was less than ten feet from the freshly mowed lawn ahead — the boundary separating the wilderness from the lodge property. Then the rain began to fall in earnest. The soft droplets ran through his hair and along his cheeks. Finch spread his arms open as if he might capture a barrelful of rain and quench his thirst directly from the cloudburst.

It was a brief moment of delight — suddenly plunged into chaos as the sound of automatic rifle fire cracked through the air. Finch dropped to the ground and onto his belly. A pause followed the first round of fire — then a brutal barrage continued the firefight. A moment later the guns fell silent.

Finch rose to his knees and studied the landscape. It's coming from the front of the lodge, he whispered to himself. And look there. Two men leaped from where they were hiding between the concrete storage hut and the A-frame. The men had been invisible, but now they sprinted across the lawn to the back of the food locker. Surprised by their quick movements, Finch admired their speed and agility bearing their weapons and armored gear.

He froze as he watched the two men pause behind the back wall to check their weapons. Their attention was absorbed by the lodge, their rifles, the sound of battle at the front of the resort. Their intense preparations suggested that some new danger was imminent. Perhaps Skipper, Claws, Dogboy, and Jasper were about to attack through the kitchen door. And they would be coming right at him.

Chapter Thirty-Five

SKIPPER CRAWLED ALONG the floor from the reception desk and through the kitchen door. As it swung shut behind him, he stood up and jogged over to the north window. To his left stood the twin steel doors of the emergency exit. He pressed the palm of his left hand on the crash bar. Tested its heft to determine if it would lever open when he charged into the backyard. "Yeah, good."

He slipped his forehead around the window sill and scanned the yard leading up to the A-frame and the forest beckoning him to safety. He could feel his blood boiling with rage, adrenaline, and the sheer glory of killing. Nice of Macron to mention that only two troops manned each exit. The information defined his next tactics. He could snipe one from the kitchen window, then run-and-gun the number two grunt.

"Fuck! You got it all, Skip!" he wailed, brushing the sweat from his face. Then he noticed the streak of blood on his hand. "What?" He swept his cheek with his fingers. He blinked. A dot of blood swam into his right eye. Something's hit your eyelid, pal. He leaned his rifle next to the door frame and carefully pulled his eyelid up and over the eyeball. But before he could release the flap of skin, a narrow stream of blood welled over his cheek and along his jaw.

"Shit!" he cried and dabbed his eye with the cuff of his shirt sleeve. Must've been the backsplash from the shattered glass when he took out Macron. He drew a breath, ducked under the window, and stood next to the right side of the window frame. With one hand covering his wound, he studied the yard with his good eye.

Ten feet past the emergency door stood a shed. A storage unit? No, the food locker. It'll provide your first cover. Beyond stood the A-frame where he knew two men were staked out. Where Finch lay dead. You snipe the first SWATer, then run-and-gun to the hut. From there it's a roll of the dice. If you control the speed, you get the kill.

He moved back to the right side of the window. He noticed the window was top-hinged with a lever handle locked to the bottom of the frame. He ducked down, released the lock, and slowly opened the bottom of the window. Two inches, just enough to fit the rifle muzzle through the slot. There'd be no backsplash this time. He stood up and shouldered his weapon, then waited until he caught a glimpse of the enemy. Despite the heavy rainfall, with one good eye, he knew any sign would do. A shadow, a glint of light. Then you shoot and run.

And there it was. A helmet shifted from left to right behind the food locker. As he fired the AR-15, he felt the rifle butt rivetting against his shoulder. He saw something fly through the air. What? *Yes.* An empty helmet tumbled onto the lawn.

One down, one to go.

Before he could slot a fresh magazine into the 15, a barrage of bullets tore through the kitchen wall. He heard the percussion of metallic pings drumming behind him as the bullets ricocheted off the kitchen appliances. The propane stove, the refrigerator, the line of steel knives and spatulas hanging from the ceiling — all of them rattling in a broken syncopation.

He dropped to the floor, clutched his weapon to his chest, and crawled toward the steel doors.

"Make your move, Skip," he whispered. *Now, while you still can.*

As he lay next to the doors Skipper struggled to reload his AR-15. With his vision fading as he worked, he grew more frantic. He counted off the seconds as his fingers dropped the magazine and then fumbled to insert it into place. Ten seconds. Twenty. Finally, he was locked and loaded.

"Now," he told himself. He hesitated again. But he knew there was no time to delay. He pulled himself to his knees and pressed his fingers to the crash bar on the steel emergency exit door

Then he doubted himself. Maybe it would be better to go back to the Rotunda and lead all thirty hostages through the front door. His rifle lined up to kill them all at once. Then grab a fast car and … what? Play it hard and fast like rock 'n' roll. Everything rough and tumble.

With a hand pressed to his wounded eye, he turned to study the hole in the wall that led from the kitchen to the toilet stall. The hole that Finch had opened up. Fucking Finch. If he crawled through the hole he could slip around the reception hall into the Rotunda without detection.

But then another hail of bullets blistered the kitchen wall and the propane stove took a direct hit. First came a spark, then a single, brilliant explosion blew the room apart.

As he barrelled through the emergency exit, he fired wild shots toward the food locker. If he could hit the second man, he'd be home free. Skipper felt the fire scorching his back. His pant leg burst into flames and he stumbled wildly toward the forest. His left arm swung in all directions as he looked for cover. He could see the food locker just ahead and a single shooter checking the pulse of his comrade.

He sprayed a full clip of bullets in a narrow arc. The last man went down. He'd won! The run 'n' gun was his! Then the flames began to overwhelm him. He threw his rifle aside and swept his arms across his shoulders in a desperate effort to brush the flames from his body. When the fire seared across his torso he let out a scream. He stopped in his tracks, bellowing in pain. When he could no longer breathe, he collapsed on his knees and let out a silent cry of outrage.

As the fire consumed him, he saw two figures standing at the forest edge. The two women. And in front of them, squatting on the ground, another man aiming a pistol at him.

Finch.

CHAPTER THIRTY-SIX

AS HE LAY flat on the ground, Finch couldn't see Skipper opening the levered kitchen window. Didn't see the muzzle of his rifle poke under the glass frame, nor the gun flash as he unloaded a full magazine at the two SWAT fighters hovering next to the concrete food locker. But he did hear the bullets zinging overhead, then the horrible cry from one of the men as a round cut through his throat.

Finch moved behind the shelter of the A-frame. From his vantage point he could see the steel exit door on the Rotunda nudge open, then close again. The door where Eve had made her escape in the middle of the night. Then the door swung wide open. Roland Clapp stepped outside and made a sweeping motion with his arm. Holding hands, a couple slipped out of the dome. Vic and Jenny Wexler. They were followed by Frank and Jeanine Winters. Then a group of five slipped free, all of them following the Wexlers who led the way past the far end of the dome and into the forest. Within seconds Clapp guided the remaining hostages through the doors and into the woods.

Seconds later the second fighter unleashed a barrage of heavy-caliber fire at the kitchen. In the time it took to draw another breath, Finch heard the massive eruption in the kitchen.

Whooom!

He felt the percussion blast through the shrubs and salal surrounding him. When the rolling flames exploded through the air, he knew the firefight would soon be over. He rose to his knees and shook his head in disbelief as he assessed the catastrophe. Within seconds the roof lit up the back of the lodge and the top of the Rotunda ignited in a roaring fireball.

Seconds later, the steel doors at the back of the kitchen flew open. Now he could see Skipper stumbling toward them. His mask off, one hand firing his rifle in a wild burst of automatic fire that sprayed across the entire yard. Then Finch saw the second fighter drop to the ground. He'd been hit in the legs and wailed in pain on the lawn between the food locker and the A-frame.

Finch's attention turned back to Skipper. He could see a tongue of flame licking up the back of his right leg and onto his shirt. He dropped his rifle and brushed a dash of blood from his eyes. Both arms windmilled around his back as he tried to extinguish the ribbons of fire now streaming from his shirt. As his clothing burst into flames, somehow Skipper managed to continue running forward.

Finch stepped over to the wounded SWAT fighter and drew the pistol from the man's holster. A Glock 20. A weapon Finch had fired more than a few times over the years. He braced the pistol in both hands and took aim at Skipper — a human torch staggering blindly in a dizzy arc. Perhaps thirty feet separated the two men. Steady and alert, Finch leveled the Glock at Skipper's chest as the terrorist dropped to his knees and let out a horrible scream.

Finch slumped onto the ground, his buttocks flush on the lawn, his legs stretched out before him, knees bent at an angle, feet flat on the wet grass. He braced his forearms on top of his knees and steadied the Glock in a two-fisted grip, the gunsight fixed on Skipper's chest. Finch waited as if he had to make a choice. Shoot the bastard to put him out of this misery, or spare himself the guilt that follows when you kill a defenseless creature.

"Will."

He turned his head. Ten feet behind him Eve stood with Brittany at her side. One of Brittany's hands covered her mouth as if she was blocking a scream.

"Will, what are you doing?"

He felt his heart swelling in his chest. She was here. They were together again. The rain poured over his head, chest, and legs.   He felt the damn breaking inside him. His anger, his pain, his desperation — everything that had been bottled up inside — all of it broke loose. Despite his exhilaration, he didn't know how to respond.

"I'm…" His voice faltered. "Just considering … the options."

He blinked and rolled his shoulders, unsure what that meant.

"What options?"

Damn it, his feet hurt. So did his belly and his wrists. "I thought maybe I should kill him. But now I'm not so sure."

"Then maybe you should put the gun down."

He had to think about that, too. He studied Skipper's body, twisting into a charred heap on the lawn. The dwindling flames struggled to climb through the downpour of rain. Then he looked at Eve again and let the pistol slip from his hands into his lap. Yes. She was right.

Better just to let Skipper burn.

CHAPTER THIRTY-SEVEN

OFFICER WAYNE MORTON passed a paper cup of coffee to Brittany, then served cups to Eve and Finch. "Good thing you take it black," he said. "We've only got the powdered stuff. And no sugar," he added.

"No problem." Finch took a sip and felt the warm liquid slide down his throat. Not bad, he thought as he studied the plumes of water spraying over the remains of the lodge. The volunteer Fire Department from Mendocino had brought their own pumper and water tender trucks to handle the blaze. Finch wondered if they had the resources to douse the fire before it tore through the forest.

However, the fire chief, Raymond Souster, was feeling confident. A total professional, he'd directed his team — all sixteen of them — to bring the fire under control within an hour. Furthermore, the flash rainstorm was heavy and the forecast called for a steady downpour over the next week.

"Rain all the way down the coast to Los Angeles," he said. "The boys with tin hats are calling it an atmospheric river," he added with an amused chuckle.

"Tin hats?" Brittany sat next to Eve under the row of tarps the SWAT team had set up on the far side of the lodge parking lot. "What does that mean?"

"Engineers, computer dweebs, rocket scientists. In this case, meteorologists." Souster smiled. "They've come up with a bunch of jargon. Heat domes. Atmospheric rivers. I guess it helps them cope with climate change."

"Well, if it can douse this fire," Morton said, "they can call it whatever they damn well like."

Finch stepped back a foot to gain more cover under the tarp. He'd just finished talking to Sergeant Conner for twenty minutes. A quick debrief, he'd called it. First, Conner interviewed Eve, then Brittany. After Finch, Roland Clapp, his wife, and all the hostages would take turns talking to the two trauma counselors who had flown in on another helicopter. All thirty survivors, along with the day staff, Michaels, Finnegan, and Salter had made it out of the Rotunda intact. Some were bruised, some battered, but otherwise, they were unscathed. More thorough interviews would follow when everyone returned to San Francisco. Finch knew it would take months before the FBI and Homeland Security could report their findings to Congress. Likely the lawsuits would drag on for years.

Conner hadn't revealed any information about the terrorists to Finch. Protocol dictated as much. Besides that, after Lieutenant Macron had been killed by Skipper, Conner had to step into the breach. Finch could see he was shaken. Nonetheless, Conner managed to conduct the interview with composure. But the conversation was a one-way street. Conner asked the questions and Finch replied with whatever information he could provide. He revealed that he'd set the fire that enabled Eve's escape. But he had to gloss over his walk in the forest with Jasper. He still hadn't fully recovered from the trauma of his mock execution. When Conner seemed satisfied, Finch tried to turn the tables.

"What about Dogboy?"

"Dogboy?"

"The man Eve turned over to you." He smiled with a conspiratorial grin to lure Conner into his confidence. "Real name, Daniel Smith."

Conner's lips pinched together. "All I can tell you is that he's on the way to the slammer in San Francisco. Most likely he'll be incarcerated in a federal prison for decades to come."

"Who were they working for?" Finch felt his inner journalist digging for any answers he could pry from the tight-lipped sergeant. Even denials were valuable. Sometimes more valuable than the facts.

"You know I can't tell you that."

Finch kept his eyes on Conner, then offered him a beggar's frown. "All right. What about your side? I know you lost Gerold Macron. Any others?"

"Yeah. Macron and two others. The man you saw take the hit behind the A-frame. And the other shot in the legs. He's been evacuated to Zuckerberg General Hospital in San Francisco. I guess there'll be a press conference in the next week or two. It'll all come out then."

"What were their names?"

"Sorry, Mr. Finch. Look, I've got to get on with this thing." He waved a hand at the charred remains of the resort, a gesture to dismiss Finch and his questions. "Maybe when the official reports are made public, we can talk again."

Finch limped over to where Eve was sitting with Brittany. They both stared at the miserable scene on the far side of the parking lot. The pumper truck spraying water through the rainstorm onto the bare-bone skeleton of the lodge. The SWAT team wrangling the hostages into a line where a makeshift galley served hot soup and bread.

He sidled up to Eve and tipped his head toward the coffee station. She stood and followed him, and when they were alone she looped her hand around his elbow and kissed his cheek.

"You okay?" She ran an index finger over the ladder of stitches above his eyebrow.

"Yeah. Gonna be, anyhow."

They hugged and surrendered to a long, tender kiss. Then he leaned back and gazed into her eyes.

"So tell me what happened."

"You mean after I slipped out of the Rotunda?"

"Yeah, from then until you found me."

She shook her head with a sullen frown. "Like I told you back at the A-frame. Jasper, Claws, Dogboy..." She waved a hand and paused. "It's a *long* story."

"Another one."

He waited for her to continue.

"Yeah." She rolled her chin to one side. "Let's sit down over there and I'll tell you everything."

They moved two camp chairs to the far edge of the tarp and

sat down side by side. Over the next hour, she told the story of her escape from the lodge, her tactical mistake of moving off the road into the forest, meeting Brittany at the burnt-out shack, the corpse they'd found — which she'd reported to Sergeant Conner — the battle with Claws, and Brittany's insulin crash. It took several false starts and hesitations to tell him the story of Claws's horrific attack on Jasper and Eve's desperation when she shot him point blank as he charged at her.

Finch took her free hand in his own as she paused to brush the tears from her cheek.

"There's no blame attached, Eve. It was self-defense." A reassuring smile crossed his lips. "You know that, right?"

She nodded. "Still. My God, Will. It's not the first time."

"I know." He released her hand and gazed into the distance. Over the years together, they'd both had to kill to survive. He let out a deep sigh. "Tell me what happened next."

Eve took a moment to recover her composure and then described the events leading to her final trek through the forest with Brittany which led to the moment when she saw Finch poised to shoot Skipper.

"You know, when I saw you sitting there on the ground, with the gun in your hand, ready to put him down, I knew what you were thinking."

"You did?"

"Yeah." She drew his hand into her own. "It wasn't about what came next. He was going to die whether the fire took him, or you put him out of his misery. It was about you not wanting any part of it anymore. The killing, I mean."

He wove his fingers through hers and locked them together.

"Yeah. That's pretty much it." He looked into her eyes. "It's not the dying that gets to me. It's the killing."

She gazed across the yard as a moment of silence slipped between them. Her lips pursed together and she nodded as if they'd made a new pact. "So no more then, right?"

"No. I'm done with it."

Her fingers tightened their grip on him. She leaned closer. Kissed him. "I don't want to let you go. Ever."

"I know. Me neither. Just the two of us. And Casey."

"The three of us."

"Yeah, all three of us," he said and stood up. "Let's go home and get her."

ENJOY D.F. Bailey's first stand-alone thriller

FIRE EYES

a W.H. Smith First Novel Award finalist.

Born by chance
Fueled by madness
Ignited by love

CHAPTER ONE

The bomb went off a little after one in the morning. It was a beautiful thing. There was blues and greens and thick yellows that blended in with the smoke to make it all look like mustard gas in some World War I movie. And the sound of it was much louder than I thought. I guess it could have been the noise alone that brought the cops. But the look of it — the colors — they were much more than I hoped for. Damn it, they were *beautiful*.

But what happened to Renee, that's something else. It was the last thing I expected. She tried to make everything so casual, carrying the bomb the way she did under her arm. First she spins around and smiles like there's no care to the world and moves up the sidewalk in her dream of ballet. She points her toe to the ground once, twice — then, as she turns on one foot, the bomb explodes and breaks the night into a thousand smoking greens and yellows and reds, with a huge blast like a rocket burst echoing off the walls of the mountains. And then it's all over before you can really see it and in the end she's worse than dead because the bomb blew everything apart. There's a crater gutted into the sidewalk and suddenly all the lights in the First City Electric building black out. A minute later there's a flicker of light in the windows and then the power surges back to life. Only the front door has any sign of damage, two windows shattered from their steel frames. And along the sidewalk, halfway up from the road, her handkerchief rests where it fell. Except for that, there's nothing left at all. Not even the baby.

Yes, *she's* the one that didn't come back. I remember her saying it would be like a war, and in a war there's always some that don't come home. I always thought she was talking about me. Specially when I put the bomb together in the lab.

"No, no," I tell her, "I'll be careful. I always tamp real careful when I'm making these things."

Making the bomb is when the Power comes into my mind. That's when the danger is worst. So I tamp the guts of it down into the shell with cotton balls. Cotton's best because it keeps the moisture of my fingers away from everything so none of the electrics can short out. And it's soft enough so I can build the most dangerous parts in a gentle way.

"Just be sure," she says and backs to the corner of the room near the mattress. She thinks she can dive under it if anything triggers accidental. She doesn't know that if something triggers she'd be dead before she could even *see* it.

"I am," I tell her, "just don't even breathe." I can hear her footsteps backing to the mattress. It's the kind of noise that gives me the Power. Everyone else backing off and there I am doing the impossible. Nobody else can touch it but me.

"Steady out your fingers," she says.

"Just quit your talking." Any interruption's like poison. Finally I tamp the last of the explosives into the canister and seal the shell off with a waterproof cap. That way I can leave it outside in a pinch and if rain comes there's no problem. Just wait her out till I'm ready. And I can either set it automatic or by remote. Hell, the remote's a dream these days. Some even do it with one of those garage closers. I heard of one guy who's triggering them with remote-control TV channel changers. That's a tough one to believe. But can't you see it? Parking a block down the road and just waiting till the cops come, then click it to channel 13 and *WHAM!* — they're goners.

But there wasn't a remote on Renee's. I should've put one in but it was her fault, because she wanted it timed for thirty-three-and-a-third minutes. Just like a record, she says. That's rule one. Never allow no one else in the lab. But she was a forceful one. She'd come in anytime she pleased and stick around and seldom do as I told her. You've got to admire that in a way, because most of these modern women's bitches are just hot air and no bras. Not Renee, though, she'd stick it out to the end whether there was shit in the hole or not.

That's why she took the shell instead of me. That and the fact she could pass the security check. It's the one thing they gave her for working there three years: a little plastic badge with her picture on one corner that pins to her shirt so they don't stick a knife in her guts just for walking in the front door after hours.

We drove there together and had the banger rolled in flannel blankets in the back seat. We even borrowed one of those baby harnesses that lock into the seat belts. If the cops stopped us then it'd look like some baby sleeping on the way home. Even cops wouldn't disturb no baby.

"Roll it up nice and easy," I tell her when we're setting out.

"It's so cute," she says, "what'll we call him?"

"Nothing. And you shouldn't fix yourself on the idea of having a kid." But to keep her happy I add on a new touch. "Or we could call it Billy Junior, if you really want to."

She starts laughing like this is the joke-of-the-week. "When you name it after yourself it shows you're egotistical."

"Nothing wrong with a little pride," I tell her as she pulls the blanket right over the baby's head so he can sleep like a newborn kitten.

We drive to the electricity offices in the Camaro. It takes about an hour and a half altogether, when you add in the time for the stop at the 7-Eleven and then the half-hour stop we made when she started crying. At least that's how it began. After that I think she went a little crazy on me. She was looking up at the stars and her whole face was wet from the tears and then she tried to explain everything between us. It's the kind of thing you don't want to dwell on. People will stop trusting you if you talk about the truth. Especially when you lay everything out person to person.

Anyway, we just about forget the bomb, it looks so much like a baby and the music blasting out of the radio is such a lure away from what we're really doing. When we get to the building she grabs it up very softly, just like a kid, under the ass and around the belly. I sit back and watch her go up the sidewalk. She starts to dance a little, like she's got one of those Fifties songs in her head, and pretends to be dancing at the prom. Christ, how ridiculous. Then a handkerchief slips from her pocket and drifts to the ground. She turns around without noticing it and pulls the baby to her chest and shows me how she's breast-feeding the newborn like a good mother should do. For a second I even think about being that little baby and sucking on the mother-nipple and how good it's got to taste.

She strides up the walk and does a little ballet turn. But it's no place to play ballerina, so I get out of the car and whisper up to her as loud as I dare.

"Stop that assin' around, Renee. Just drop the baby off and stop that jerk-off stuff."

She smiles that devilish smile she uses when she knows she's gone one step farther than I ever would. It's like a contest between us. Sometimes we'll try to out-chicken the other. When someone finally backs off, it shows where all the nerves really are. The winner gets to leer it into the loser and it's a big deal until the next time comes. Then it's really up to the loser. He's gotta *shine*.

But with this baby there shouldn't be no goof-assing. I've seen guys lose anything from their fingers to their life in one sudden flash. It'd be so quick you'd blink to shut it away, then open your eyes and the whole world has changed. A guy dead here. One guy with a hand off there. Maybe another guy with his stomach ripped open and his kidney flopped onto the ground. And it happens from no cause at all. Maybe God says, "Okay, now you blow up those combat engineers in F-squad. Them soldiers don't matter no more." Then the bomb just flashes and it's over.

"Gentle that baby," I whisper, "until you get inside."

Then she smiles more heavenly than I've ever seen. The Devil part turns into something sweet and she does another ballerina turn along the sidewalk.

And that's where it blows. The gas colors pour out like mustard steam and for some reason my eyes don't blink at all. They just suck it in like a mind volcano so I get to see everything flying apart.

First her smile washes out. Those angel lips fall off like the great hotels dropped by the real demolition experts. They're there one second and the next they're just gone. The whole wall of her face, smooth and clear as it is, turns into rubble and falls onto itself until there's nothing left but a pile of broken bricks and bones. There's no look of sadness, no idea that the end has come.

I run up the sidewalk after the first shock passes and look into the smoldering crater. I'm balanced there on the sidewalk, on my toes with one knee bent forward, like a wild deer in the forests ready to disappear into the night bush. But something pulls me in closer, down to where her body should be. The Devil is flying out of her and I squat over and take a good sniff of the blasting powders steaming up from the pit, then I look around and see everything perfectly. The brown brick building with two shattered front windows, the parked car, the grass and sidewalk, those prickle bushes next to the link fence. I know *exactly* how to run and break away like that deer in the woods, straight down the sidewalk jumping the lawns and shrubs, I hop the last bush and duck into the car and close the door tight and just listen. If there's squad cars coming you sit tight and tell 'em sweet dick when they ask. But if there's no cops then turn the key soft and pull out as sweet as you please.

And it works just like that. There's no sign of a soul, so I pull out unnoticeable. I dump the baby harness off at the welfare office and no one knows the difference. It's somebody's free donation. Far as they're concerned, some big-heart left it without a trace. They might even give up a prayer in the morning. Who knows how they think it through?

Then I drive round like a bug that just found some dead squirrel. Don't know where to go. Just take all the green lights and whenever there's a red one turn right and keep going. After a while I sort of come to, come right out of this automatic driving and realize how useless it is. Following the lights is crazy cause no one ever took the time to organize it so the lights'll take you somewhere. They don't lead nowhere. Just around.

Then I figure, okay, let's drive back to the building and see what's going on. It's an hour later and I'll just be a guy driving by on his own time. A guy who couldn't sleep specially well and is out for a simple drive. Even at two in the morning that's not so suspicious.

But it's like pulling the plug in a washtub that's full to the top with dirty water. At first, nobody knows the drain's free. Then a minute later the water starts sucking down and the surface rolls back and forth until the whirlpool starts. That's when you know it'll never stop and you can see the tiniest speck caught on the edge, right on the lip of the whirlpool at the one point just after any possible escape. There you are. On the lip. Right on the lip. Then one, two quick swirls and down into the guts of some black animal with no eyes. That's how it is driving back there — a dizzy hell.

When I'm a block away I can see the place has gone crazy with cops. There's at least six squad cars with their lights flashing all blue-red, like the Devil's still with Renee.

I slip the car into neutral and pull up at a coast. They've got a roadblock set up, and two cars ahead of me a cop has his nose poked through the window, yapping at the driver. I take a good clean breath.

After a minute the cop motions for me to unroll my window.

"Evenin'," he says.

"What's the trouble, officer?" I crane my neck and make sure I look surprised to see a roadblock set up so late at night.

"Routine." Then he turns more serious. "What brings you by here tonight?"

"Just out for a drive. Changed my shift today and I couldn't sleep so good."

"Let's see your license and registration," he says.

I lean over to the glovebox to get the papers and he sticks his head in all the way and starts sniffing the air. You hear him do it twice. Sniff-sniff, just like Porky Pig.

He holds the papers and license in one hand and checks my face against the picture, asks my name and address and checks my answers against the card. Then he goes to a squad car and makes some notes and radios into headquarters and lingers around his car a while.

If they had the brains for it they might've read my thoughts while I was waiting in the car lineup. But that's not too likely. Usually cops aren't good enough to read your thoughts. Not like the shrinks and special doctors. With a little training some of them could maybe handle it, but on the whole the cops are useless buggers. They're much better at reading how you sweat or how your eyes twitch if there's any little pressure inside you. And that's what I'm doing my best to control. My face is smooth as ice. It's just now that the sweat's starting to come into my palms.

"Okay, on your way."

"Thanks."

He passes the papers to me. I roll the window back up and take a deep breath. With the window up it's like sealing him off and turning him into something stupid and ignorant. Like a cartoon.

Then I drive off slow, obeying all the traffic rules as though I just took my driver's test. When I get close to it I look up the sidewalk to see Renee. But the funny thing is that there's hardly any sign of the bomb. They put a few barriers around the crater, but apart from that there's nothing. Even the building lights are lit up like nothing ever happened. You almost wonder why the cops bothered to show up.

But it's probably another trick of theirs to lure me out of what's really happened. It's the kind of trick that might work on anybody else. It might work on me, too, except that my memory's near perfect and I remember *every* little detail. Up to a point, anyhow.

About the Author

In 2015 D. F. (Don) Bailey published The Finch Trilogy — Bone Maker, Stone Eater, Lone Hunter — three novels narrated from the point-of-view of a crime reporter in contemporary San Francisco. Following the trilogy's success, Second Life (2017) launched a new saga based on the characters introduced in the first three books. The series prequel, Five Knives, came out in 2018. The Finch chronicle continues with Open Chains (2019), Run Time (2020), White Sphere (2022), and Burnt Embers (2023).

His first psychological thriller, Fire Eyes, was a W.H. Smith First Novel Award finalist. His second novel, Healing the Dead, was translated into German as Todliche Ahnungen. The Good Lie (2008) is set in his adopted hometown, Victoria. His fourth novel, Exit from America, appeared in 2013.

After his birth in Montreal, Don's family moved around North America from rural Ontario to New York City, Mississippi, and New Jersey. "After years of seeking the ideal place to live," he says, "I finally landed on my feet on Vancouver Island — where I live next to the Salish Sea in the city of Victoria."

For twenty-two years, he worked at the University of Victoria, teaching creative writing and journalism and coordinating the Professional Writing Cooperative Education Program — which he co-founded. From time to time, he also freelanced as a business writer and journalist. In the fall of 2010, Don left the university so that, "I could turn my preoccupation with writing into a full-blown obsession."

An Amazon bestselling author, he's also a ManyBooks.com Book-of-The-Month Award winner and a Whistler Independent Book Award finalist.

Subscribe to D. F. Bailey's newsletter: www.dfbailey.com

Books by D. F. Bailey

• Will Finch Mystery Thriller Series •

Bone Maker

Stone Eater

Lone Hunter

Second Life

Open Chains

Run Time

Five Knives

White Sphere

Burnt Embers

• Stand-Alone Thrillers •

Fire Eyes

Healing The Dead

The Good Lie

Exit From America

ACKNOWLEDGEMENTS

Once again I owe a debt of gratitude to Lawrence Russell who read an early draft of Burnt Embers. His insights and advice helped to shape the final version of the novel. I'm also indebted to Victor Sogen Hori for his diligent copy editing — and to the team of proofreaders who scoured the text for grammar, typos, and wayward errors: Diane Bryant, Barbara Turkdal, Bruce Tamanaha, Phil Van Itallie, Marc Brown, Paul Natale, Jeffrey R. McMillan, Joanne Lawson, Sally Forstner, and Barb Stoner.

I am especially grateful to four individuals who helped me understand the ravages and management of diabetes: Diane Bryant, Barbara Turkdal, Joanne Lawson, and Teresa Collins. In some instances, however, I dramatized the nature of diabetes to enhance the narrative tempo. Consequently, any false notes are entirely my fault. As of 2019, diabetes afflicted 537 million people worldwide. One day we will have a cure. May that day come tomorrow. — DFB

Subscribe to D. F. Bailey's newsletter: www.dfbailey.com

Manufactured by Amazon.ca
Bolton, ON

35205468R00146